A BRAVE COSSACK . . .
AN IMPOSSIBLE LOVE

"O my love!" cried Andrei, his heart and soul brimming over with emotion. Three fields are mine, half of my father's droves of horses, all that my mother brought my father—all is mine! And all this I will renounce, throw away at one word from you!"

And this Cossack was lost. Lost to all Cossack knighthood! Never again would he see his father's fields—the church of his God! Old Taras Bulba will tear from his scalp a tuft of his grey hair and curse the day and the hour when he begot a son to shame him.

☆ ☆ ☆ ☆ ☆

Nicolai Gogol's brilliant novel of fiery battle and searing emotion, TARAS BULBA, remains one of the world's all-time classics.

This new translation is designed especially for modern readers.

TARAS
BULBA

NICOLAI GOGOL

Translated by
BERNARD FARBAR

PRESTIGE BOOKS • NEW YORK

TARAS BULBA

PRESTIGE BOOKS INC. • 18 EAST 41ST STREET
NEW YORK, N.Y. 10017

ABOUT THIS BOOK

NICOLAI VASILYEVICH GOGOL (1809-1852) wrote his epic *Taras Bulba* over a period, broken by intervals, of more than nine years: from 1833 to 1842. The Ukrainian People's struggle for their independence, waged throughout the 16th and 17th centuries, stirred and inspired Gogol, a great patriot of his country. He was an enthusiastic reader of chronicles recording the events of that epoch, and loved to listen to the Ukrainian legends and historical folk ballads.

"Songs are my joy, my life! How I love them!" wrote Gogol. "Every song is a piece of folk history, living, vivid, full of color, truth, revealing the whole life of a people"; it is of priceless use to a writer who would "feel out the spirit of a bygone age."

Historical writings, legends, folk ballads and songs—all these helped Gogol to paint a realistic picture of the life of the Ukrainian people and their heroic struggle, which was particularly intensified after the year 1569.

In 1569 the Ukraine was made a part of Poland. The powerful Polish magnates took possession of the vast Ukrainian lands and ruthlessly exploited the peasants, enforced their own Polish way of life, outlawing the Ukrainian language and stamping out Ukrainian culture in their effort to enslave the Ukrainian people spiritually, sever them from Russia, and thus rob the Ukraine of its independence. The Church Union, enacted in Brest in 1596, added religious oppression to economic, political and national enslavement. The Polish priests and magnates introduced by force the Catholic faith and Papal supremacy and severely persecuted all "heretics" —adherents of the Orthodox Greek Church. All this met with fierce resistance and rebellions on the part of the Ukrainian serfs.

The history of this struggle owes much, in a progressive sense, to the Cossacks of the Zaporozhian Setch—a military brotherhood made up of serfs who fled from their lords to the rich southern lands of the Russian state, and of free men who flocked to the Setch in the hope of escaping the double yoke of national and social oppression. For many decades the Zaporozhian Cossacks took part in campaigns for their country's liberation, and were the terror of the Turks, Tatars, and Polish squires.

The Zaporozhian Cossack, Taras Bulba is a typical representative of the freedom-loving Ukrainian people. He reflected the hopes and aspirations of the Ukrainian people who dreamed of reuniting with their blood-brothers, the Russian people, who had preserved their statehood. This union Cossacks like Taras Bulba regarded as the sole means of preserving their nation and therein lies the objective historical value of Gogol's tale.

The profound ideological message of the tale, its thrilling and truthful characters, Gogol's colorful portrayal of the people's life, have immortalized Gogol's epic.

BERNARD FARBAR

CHAPTER ONE

"WELL, TURN around, son! What a scarecrow you are! What sort of a priest's cassock have you got on? Is that the way they all dress at the Academy?"

With these words did old Bulba greet his two sons, who, after finishing their education at the Kiev Seminary, had returned home.

His sons had just dismounted from their horses. They were big fellows; both of them looked bashful, as young collegians sometimes do. Their firm, healthy faces were covered in places with fuzz, which had, as yet, never been shaved. They were greatly embarrassed by such a welcome, and stood quite still with their eyes fixed on the ground.

"Stay! Let me have a good look at you," he went on, turning them round. "What long coats you have on! What coats indeed! The world has never seen their like before. Just run a little, one of you! I would like to see if you do not get tangled up in the skirts and fall down."

"Don't laugh at us, Father, don't laugh!" said the elder son at last.

"Look how proud he is! And why shouldn't I laugh?"

"Because, though you are my father, if you laugh, by God, I will give you a beating!"

"What! You ungrateful son! You would thrash your own father?" cried Taras Bulba, falling back in amazement.

"What if you are my father? I will allow no one to insult me."

"And how would you fight me? With your fists, eh?"

"Any way."

"Well, let it be with fists, then," said Taras Bulba, pulling up his sleeves. "I will see what sort of a man you are with your fists!"

And father and son, instead of a pleasant greeting after long separation, began to pommel each other on ribs, stomach and chest, now retreating and eyeing each other, then attacking again.

"Look everyone! their father has gone mad he's out of his mind!" cried the boys' thin pale-faced mother, who was standing in the doorway, and had not yet had time to greet her children. "The children are just home—for more than a year we have not seen them; and he takes it into his head to start fighting with them!"

"Why, he fights pretty well!" said Bulba, pausing. "By God, he fights well!" he continued, patting down his clothes. "So well that perhaps I'd better not have fought him at all. He will make a good Cossack! Well, son, welcome home! You can give your father a kiss now!" And father and son fell to kissing each other. "That's right, son! Thrash everyone as you've drubbed me! Give quarter to none! But your clothes are funny all the same. What rope is this dangling here? And you, you fool, why do you stand there with your hands hanging idle?" he called, turning to the youngest. "Come now, young son, aren't you going to give me a drubbing?"

"That's all you can think of!" cried the mother, who was already hugging her youngest. "Who ever heard of children fighting their own father? As if he has nothing better to do now: he's just a child, he has come ever so far, he is tired . . ." The child was over twenty, and a good six feet tall. "He ought to be resting and eating something, and you want to make him fight!"

"Ah, you're a boy, I see!" said Bulba. "Don't listen to your mother, sonny: she is a woman, and knows nothing. Do you want to be a baby all your life? The open field and a good horse—that's the kind of life you'll live! Look at this sabre—that's your mother! It's all rubbish they rammed into your heads—the Academy, and all your books and teachers, and philosophy, and the devil knows what; I spit upon it all! I had better send you next week to Zaporozhye. That's where you'll get all the education you need. There's a school for you; there alone will you get brains!"

"Are they to stay only a week at home?" the gaunt old woman asked mournfully, with tears in her eyes. "The poor boys will have no time to celebrate their homecoming, no time to get to know their own home, and I'll have no time to feast my eyes on them!"

"Be quiet with your whining, old woman! A Cossack's not made to spend his life with women. You would like to hide both of them under your petticoats, and sit upon them as a hen sits on eggs. Go now, go, and put everything you have in the house on the table. We want none of your dumplings, honey-cakes, poppy seed rolls, none of your pastry. Give us a whole sheep, a goat, forty-year-old mead; yes, and plenty of vodka, not with your cakes, your raising and rubbish, but pure, foamy vodka that sparkles and hisses madly."

Bulba led his sons into the best room of the house, where two pretty maidservants wearing red necklaces (who had been putting the house in order) ran out hastily. They were either frightened by the arrival of the young men, who were so strict with everybody, or else they merely wanted to keep up the feminine custom of screaming and flying at the sight of a man, and then covering their blushing faces with their sleeves. The room was furnished in the taste of that period, a period surviving only in songs and folk legends which are no longer sung in the Ukraine by the blind, bearded old minstrels, who used to sing them to the soft strumming of the *bandura*, surrounded by crowds of country-folk, when the Ukraine was fighting her first battles against the Union of the Greek Church with the Pope. The walls, floor, and ceiling were neatly plastered with colored clay. The walls were hung with sabres, riding-whips, bird and fish nets, guns, a fancy, inlaid powder-horn, a golden horse's bit, and tether-ropes with silver fastenings. The windows in the room were small, with dim, round-cut panes, such as are now found only in ancient churches, and through which one could only see by raising the sash. The windows and doors were rimmed with red. On shelves in the corners stood ewers, flasks, and flagons of green and blue glass, carved silver goblets, and gilded cups of all manner of workmanship—Venetian, Turkish, Circassian, which had found their way into Bulba's possession by various ways, a thing quite common in those adventurous days. The elmwood benches, which ran all round the room; the huge table in the front corner, under the icons; the wide stove with its many nooks and projections, laid out with various colored glazed tiles, with stove-ledges between the stove and the wall—all this was familiar enough to the two boys, who had every year walked home for the holidays. Yes, walk they did, for they had no horses of their own yet and because it was not the custom to permit college students to ride on horseback. They had nothing except their long hair to show for their manhood, and this every Cossack wearing arms was entitled to pull. It was only upon graduation that Bulba sent them a pair of young stallions from his herd.

In honor of his sons' return, Bulba had summoned all the *sotniks* and all the officers of his regiment who happened to be at home; and when two of them came together with his old comrade Captain Dmitro Tovkach, he immediately presented his sons to them, saying, "See what fine lads they are! I shall send them to the Setch very soon." The guests congratulated Bulba as well as the two boys and said that they were doing the right thing, that there was no better school for a young man than the Zaporozhian Setch.

"Well, brother officers, sit at the table. Now, sons, first let us drink some vodka!" said Bulba. "God's blessing be upon us! Here's to your health, my sons; to yours, Ostap, and to yours, Andrei. God grant you luck in war, may you beat all misbelievers; Turks, and Tatars, and Poles, too—if the Poles begin anything against our faith. Well, push up your cups; isn't the vodka good? And what is the Latin for vodka? Ah, there you are, son; the Latins were fools: they did not even know there was vodka in the world. What was the name of the fellow who wrote Latin verses? I'm not much of a scholar, so I'm not sure—was it Horace?"

"That's just like him!" thought the elder son, Ostap. "He knows everything, the old dog, yet pretends to know nothing."

"I suppose the Archimandrite did not let you have so much as a whiff of vodka," Taras went on. "Confess now, my boys, did they not lash you good and proper with fresh cherry-rods about the back and everything else a Cossack has? And perhaps, when you grew too clever, they even flogged you

10

with whips? And not only on Saturdays, I should think, but on Wednesdays and Thursdays also?"

"It's no good talking about the past," Ostap coolly answered. "What has been is done with."

"Let anyone try it now," said Andrei, "let any man touch me now! Why, as soon as I catch sight of a Tatar, I'll show him what manner of thing a Cossack sabre is!"

"Well said, son, well said, by God! And since it's come to that, I'm going with you, too! By God, I am. What the devil should I stay here for? Become a sower of buckwheat, a housekeeper, tend sheep and swine, and wear my wife's petticoats? The plague take her! I am a Cossack; I'll have none of it! What if there is no war now? I'll go with you to Zaporzhye just the same and make merry there. By God, I will!" And old Bulba grew warmer and warmer until finally, having worked himself into a real rage, he rose from the table, struck a dignified pose, and stamped his foot. "We will go tomorrow! Why should we put if off? What enemy can we await here? What do we want with this hut? What are all these things to us? What do we want with these pots?" With these words he began to smash the pitchers and flasks and to hurl them on the ground.

The poor old woman, well used to her husband's ways, remained seated on a bench and watched him sadly. She did not dare say anything; but when she heard the decision which she dreaded so much, she could not keep back her tears; she gazed at the children she was doomed so soon to part with, and the force of mute despair which seemed to quiver in her eyes and convulsively compressed lips defied all description.

Bulba was featfully stubborn. He was one of those characters who first emerged in the grim fifteenth century, in a half-nomadic corner of Europe, when the whole of primitive Southern Russia, deserted by its princes, was laid waste and burned to the ground by the irresistible incursions of Mongolian spoilers; when, robbed of house and home, men grew daring; when they settled on the ashes of their homes, amidst formidable foes and perpetual perils, and grew used to looking them straight in the face and forgot there was such a thing as fear in the world; when a warlike flame fired the Slavonic spirit, which had remained peaceable for centuries, and begot Cossackdom—a free, riotous outgrowth of the Russian character—and when all the river-banks, fords and ferries, and every suitable spot in the river country, were sown with Cossacks, whose number no man knew; and as their bold comrades answered the Sultan, who asked how many there were. "Who knows! We are spread over all the area: on every hillock will you find a Cossack." This was a remarkable manifestation of Russian strength, out of dire misfortune. Instead of the old principalities and small towns, crowded with huntsmen and laborers, instead of the petty princes, who warred and bartered their towns amongst themselves, there sprang up formidable settlements and embattled *kurens* bound together by common danger and common hatred of the raiders. As we all know from history, it was their incessant struggle and adventurous spirit that saved Europe from the savage incursions which threatened to overwhelm her. The kings of Poland, who became the sovereigns, albeit weak and remote, of these vast lands in place of the worthless princes, realized the value of the Cossacks and the advantages of their warlike, vigilant mode of life. They flattered them and encouraged their ways. Under their remote rule, the Hetmans, chosen from amongst the Cossacks themselves, transformed the settlements and *kurens* into regiments and military districts. This was not a regular standing army; there was no trace of it; but in the event of war it took only eight days for every man to appear horsed, armed from head to foot, and ready to serve at one word from the king; and in two weeks' time such an army was gathered as no regular craft could have ever banded together. Once the campaign was over, the warrior went back to his field or pasture, to the ferries, took himself fishing, trading, or brewing beer, and was once more a free Cossack. Correctly did their foreign contemporaries marvel at their singular aptitude. There was no craft the Cossack did not know: he could make wine, build a cart, grind powder, do a blacksmith's and a locksmith's work, and besides all this he could revel in the most riotous manner, could drink and feast as only a Russian can —all this he could do and more. Besides the *registered* Cossacks, whose duty it was to join the army in case of war, troops of mounted volunteers could always be mustered in time of urgent need. The town-criers had but to make a round of the market-places and squares of all the villages and towns, and there, standing up in a cart, to shout at the top of their voices:

"Ho, you beer-brewers and wine-makers! Have done with your beer-brewing, your dawdling on stove-ledges, feeding the flies with your fat carcasses! Come and win knightly fame and honor! And you farmers, you sowers of buckwheat, you tenders of sheep, you lovers of women! Have done with following the plough and mucking up your yellow boots with mud; have done with running after women and wasting your knightly strength! The hour is come to win Cossack glory!"

And these were as sparks falling on dry wood. The ploughman broke his plough, the wine-makers and beer-brewers threw away their vats and shattered their barrels, the craftsman and merchant sent their craft and shop to the devil and smashed the pots in their houses. And every man mounted his horse. In short, the Russian character displayed itself at its greatest and mightiest here.

Taras was one of the original, old colonels, born with a restless, fighting spirit and known for his blunt and straightforward manner. In those times, Polish influences had already begun to tell upon the Russian nobility. Many of the nobles were adopting Polish customs, introducing luxuries, magnificent suites, falcons, huntsmen, banquets, courts. This was not to Bulba's taste. He loved the simple life of the Cossacks, and fell out with those of his comrades who inclined toward the Warsaw party, calling them minions of the Polish lords. An indefatigable soul, he counted himself a rightful defender of the Orthodox faith. He would ride of his own accord into any village which complained of oppression by the leaseholders or of a fresh chimney tax, and, aided by his Cossacks, would execute justice. He laid down the rule that the sabre was to be drawn on three occasions—when the Polish tax-collectors did not pay due respect to the Cossack elders and stood with covered heads in their presence; when the Orthodox faith was abused or an ancestral custom violated; and lastly, when the foes were Mussulman or Turk, against whom he considered it justifiable under any circumstances to take up arms for the glory of Christendom.

Now he rejoiced beforehand at the thought of how he would turn up at the Setch with his sons and say, "See what fine young men I've brought you!" how he would introduce them to all his old, battle-tried comrades; how he would behold their first feats in the art of war and in carousing, which he counted among the principal knightly qualities. At first he had intended to send them by themselves, but the sight of their freshness, their tall stature, and their strong manly

13

beauty inflamed his warlike spirit, and he resolved to ride with them himself on the morrow, although it was only his own stubborn will which had prompted the decision. He was already busy giving orders, choosing horses and trappings for his young sons, going into stables and storehouses, and picking the servants who were to accompany them the next day. He delegated his authority to Esaul Tovkach together with the strict injunction to lead the regiment to the Setch the moment he sent for it. He forgot nothing, although he was drunk, the vodka fumes still lingering in his head. He even gave orders that the horses should be watered and their cribs filled with the best large-grained wheat. He was quite tired out by all this work when he returned.

"Well, children, we must sleep now, and tomorrow we shall do what God wills. Don't bother about beds, old wife; we will sleep in the open."

Night had just embraced the heavens, but Bulba always retired early. He threw himself down on a rug and covered himself with a long sheepskin coat, because the night air was rather fresh and because he liked to sleep warm when at home. He soon began to snore, and everyone in the yard followed his example; a medley of snores rose from the different corners where they lay; the first to fall asleep was the watchman, for he had drunk more than anyone else in honor of the young masters' home-coming.

The poor mother alone did not sleep. She bent over her sons' heads as they lay side by side, she combed their carelessly tangled curls and moistened them with her tears. She gazed at them with all her soul in her eyes, with all her senses, nay, with all her being turned into sight, and yet she could not gaze her fill. She had fed them at her own breast—she had cherished them—she had reared them—and now she was seeing them only for an instant! "My sons, my darling sons! What will become of you? What fate awaits you?" she moaned, and tears quivered in the wrinkles which had changed her once fair face. And, in truth, she was miserable, as was every woman in those fierce times. Only for a brief moment had she lived for love, only in the first heat of passion, in the first flush of youth; and then her stern husband had forsaken her for his sabre, his comrades, and his carousing. She would see him but for two or three days after a year's absence and then would hear nothing of him for years. And what a life was hers when she did see him, when they lived together! She endured insults and even blows; the rare caresses that she saw were nothing but charity. She was a strange creature amidst that community of wifeless knights. Her joyless youth flitted by and her beautiful fresh cheeks and bosom lost their bloom, unkissed, and became faded and wrinkled before their time. All her love, all her feelings, everything that is tender and ardent in a woman, was turned into one feeling—a mother's love. She hovered over her children like the gull of the steppes, full of passion and pain. Her sons, her darling sons were being taken away from her, and, perhaps, she would never see them again! Who can say—perhaps the Tatar will cut off their heads in their very first battle, and she will not know where their forsaken bodies lie; perhaps they will be torn to pieces by vultures; and yet for a single drop of their blood she would give all that was hers in the world. Sobbing, she gazed into their eyes, which all-powerful sleep was beginning to seal, and thought, "Ah, would that Bulba, when he wakes, put off their departure for a day or two; perhaps he has made up his mind to ride so soon from having drunk too much."

The moon shining high in the heavens had long since lighted up the whole yard, filled with sleeping Cossacks, the thick clump of willows and the tall weeds that drowned the palisade surrounding the yard. She still sat at her darling sons' heads, never taking her eyes off them for a moment, nor thinking of sleep. Already the horses, sensing the approach of dawn, had ceased champing and lay down upon the grass; the topmost leaves of the willows began to whisper, and little by little the whispering streamed down to the lowest branches. She sat there till daylight, not at all weary and wishing in her heart that the night might last on and on. From the steppe came the ringing neigh of a colt; bright-red streaks flashed across the sky.

Bulba suddenly awoke and sprang to his feet. He remembered quite well what orders he had given the night before.

"Now, my lads, you've slept enough! 'tis time! Water the horses! Where's the old wife? Hurry, old wife, get us something to eat—a long road lies before us."

The poor old woman, her last hope gone, dragged herself sadly indoors. While she tearfully prepared everything for breakfast, Bulba gave his orders to one and all, bustled about in the stables, and himself chose the best trappings for his children. The collegians were suddenly transformed: instead

15

of their muddy high-boots each was now shod in red morocco ones with silver-rimmed heels; the trousers, wide as the Black Sea, and with a thousand folds and pleats, were girded with a golden cord; from this cord hung long thongs with tassels. Their *cossackins*, of a fiery-red cloth, were held tight at the waist by ornamented sashes, into which were thrust engraved Turkish pistols; sabres clanked at their heels. Their faces, scarcely sunburnt as yet, seemed handsomer and fairer; their youthful black moustaches set off the whiteness of their skin, rich with all the health and sturdiness of youth; they looked very handsome under their caps of black sheepskin with crowns of gold cloth. Poor mother! When she saw them she could not utter a word, and tears welled up in her eyes.

"Now, my sons, all is ready, let's not waste time!" said Bulba at last. "But first, as our Christian custom bids us, we must all sit down before our journey."

Everyone sat down, including the serving men, who had been standing respectfully at the door.

"Now bless your children, Mother!" said Bulba. "Pray God that they may fight bravely, that they might ever defend their knightly honor, and ever stand for the faith of Christ. And if not—may they perish and leave no trace on earth! Go up to your mother, children; a mother's prayer saves a man on land and sea."

The mother, weak as all mothers, embraced them, took two small icons, and hung them, sobbing, round their necks.

"May the Mother of God . . . keep you. . . . Forget not your mother, my sons . . . send me word of yourselves . . ." She could say no more.

"Well, children, let us go!" said Bulba.

The horses stood saddled at the door. Bulba sprang upon his Devil, who shied wildly aside as he felt on his back the tremendous weight of his rider, for Taras was remarkably heavy and stout.

When the mother saw that her sons had also mounted, she rushed towards the younger, whose features wore a softer expression; she gripped his stirrup, clung to the saddle, and, with despair in her eyes, would not let him out of her hands. Two burly Cossacks gently picked her up and carried her into the hut. But when they had ridden through the gateway, she ran out after them, in spite of her years as swift as a wild goat, stopped the horse with incredible strength, and threw her arms round one of her sons with mad, uncontrollable passion. She was led away again. The young Cossacks rode on with heavy hearts, keeping back their tears for fear of their father, who was also somewhat shaken, although he strove not to show it. It was a bleak day, but there was a hard glint in the steppe grass, and the birds seemed to twitter all out of tune. Presently they looked back: their hamlet seemed to have sunk into the earth; they could see nothing above the ground but the two chimneys of their house and the tops of the trees whose branches they had once climbed like squirrels. And then only the distant field was to be seen—the field that brought to mind all the years of their lives, from the time when they had rolled in its dew-drenched grass to the time when each had waited there for a dark-browed Cossack lass, who timidly flew across it on quick young feet. And now only the solitary pole above the well with a cart-wheel fastened to its top stands etched against the sky; and the plain behind them looks from afar like a mountain hiding everything from view.

Farewell childhood, farewell games, and everything, and everyone—all!

CHAPTER TWO

ALL THREE horsemen rode in silence. Old Taras was thinking of days long gone by: before him passed his youth, those
bygone years—the years over which every Cossack weeps,
for he would like his whole life to be youth. He wondered
whom of his old comrades-in-arms he would meet at the
Setch. He reckoned up those who were dead and those he
hoped were still alive. A tear dimmed his eye, and his grey
head bent sadly.

His sons were thinking of other things. But first more
should be said about them. At the age of twelve they had
been sent to the Kiev Academy, for in those times all men of
high standing deemed it their duty to give their sons an education—if only to have them forget afterwards everything
they learned. At first, like all who entered the college, they
were wild, brought up in lawlessness, but while there they
acquired a certain polish, which, being common to all collegians, made them resemble one another. The elder, Ostap,
began his career by running away the very first year. He was
brought back, unmercifully flogged, and put to his books.
Four times did he bury his primer in the ground, and four
times was he given a brutal trouncing and a new primer. No
doubt he would have buried the fifth, too, had not his father

solemnly promised to put him into a monastery and keep him there for a full twenty years as a novice, and sworn in advance that he should never lay eyes on Zaporozhye unless he learned all the sciences taught in the Academy. It is an odd thing that the man who said this was the very same Taras Bulba who ranted against all learning and advised his children to give no thought to it at all. But from that time Ostap pored over his dull books with a rare assiduity and soon was one of the best students.

Education in those days was hopelessly at variance with the actual way of life; all the scholastic, grammatical, rhetorical, and logical subtleties were decidedly out of touch with the times and wholly without use in life. The students could not apply their knowledge, even the least scholastic, to anything whatever. The tutors themselves were even more incapable than the rest by reason of their total divorcement from practice. At the same time the republican structure of the Academy, the fearful mass of hale and hearty young men, could not but lead the collegians to activities quite outside the curriculum. Ill-treatment, oft-repeated punishments by hunger, the many impulses that arise in a fresh and strong lad—all this led to the burgeoning of an enterprising spirit which afterwards flourished in Zaporozhye. The hungry collegians prowling the streets of Kiev were a constant menace to its citizens. The bazaar-women, when they caught sight of a passing collegian, always covered their pies, *bubliks*, and pumpkin seeds with their hands, in the manner an eagless protects her young. The *consul*, whose duty it was to keep an eye on his school-fellows, himself had such frightful trouser-pockets that he could have stowed in them the whole of a gaping bazaar-woman's stall.

These collegians formed an entirely separate world; they were not admitted to the higher circles, which were composed of Russian and Polish nobility. The Waywode himself, Adam Kisel, though a patron of the Academy, ordered them to be kept out of society and under strict supervision. This last injunction, however, was quite superfluous, for neither the rector nor the monk-professors spared rod or whip; and often at their command the instructors flogged their *consuls* with such gusto that the latter scratched their trousers for weeks afterwards. To many this was a mere trifle and seemed but a little stronger than good vodka with a dash of pepper; others, at length, wearied of being dressed constantly with such poultices and fled to Zaporozhye—if they managed to find the road and were not caught on the way.

Ostap Bulba, although he applied himself assiduously to logic and even theology, did not escape the inexorable rod. Naturally, all this could not but harden his character and give him that toughness which has always distinguished the Cossacks. Ostap was generally acknowledged as the best of men. He rarely led his fellows in such adventurous enterprises as raiding a private orchard or garden, but he was always among the first to join the colors of any enterprising collegian, and never, under any circumstance, did he betray his comrades. No rods or whips could make him do so. He frowned at any temptations save those of fighting and carousing; at least, he rarely if ever gave thought to anything else. He was single-hearted with his equals. He was kind—as kind as a man of his mettle could be in his time. He was genuinely moved by the tears of his poor mother, and that was the only thing that now saddened him and made him hang his head in thought.

The sentiments of his younger brother Andrei were somewhat livelier and maturer. He learned more willingly and without the effort usually required of a strong and heavy character. He was more inventive than his brother and more often the leader of rather hazardous enterprises; his ready wit sometimes helped him to escape chastisement, while his brother Ostap, despising subterfuges, threw off his coat and lay down on the floor, without ever thinking of begging for mercy. Andrei, too, burned with the thirst for heroic deeds, but his heart was open to other feelings as well. When he had passed his eighteenth year, a longing for love blazed up within him. Woman began to appear more often in his ardent dreams; while listening to philosophical debates, he would still see her—fresh, dark-eyed, gentle. Ever before him were her glimmering firm bosom, her beautiful soft arm, bare to the shoulder; the very gown that clung to her maidenly yet powerful limbs seemed inexpressibly voluptuous in his dreams. He carefully concealed these yearnings of his passionate young soul from his fellows, for in that age it was a shame and dishonor for a Cossack to think of woman and love before he had gone to the wars. During his last years at the Academy he had rarely been leader of adventurous bands, but more frequently had wandered alone in the remote corners of Kiev, where low-roofed houses, buried in cherry orchards, peeped alluringly into the street. He had also ventured into the aristocratic quarter, which is now Old Kiev, where the Ukrainian and Polish nobles used to dwell and where the houses were built in a more fanciful style.

Once, as he stood there gaping, he was nearly run over by some Polish nobleman's coach, and the frightfully mustachioed driver, sitting on the box, gave him a well-aimed cut with his whip. The young collegian flew into a rage: with thoughtless daring he seized a hind wheel with his powerful hand and stopped the coach. The coachman, fearing a reprisal, laid his whip on his horses; they broke into a gallop, and Andrei, who had fortunately withdrawn his hand in time, fell face downwards in the mud. The sweetest and most musical of laughs resounded above him. He looked up and saw, standing at a window, a beautiful girl such as he had never beheld before—dark-eyed and white as snow tinged with the rosy dawn. She was laughing with all her heart, and her laughter enhanced her dazzling beauty. He stood spell-bound. He stared at her in utter confusion, absently wiping the mud off his face, which only made it dirtier. Who was the beautiful girl? He sought to elicit that information from the servants, who, in rich liveries, stood at the gate in a crowd around a young *balalaika* player. But they laughed at the sight of his grimy face and did not reply. At length he learned that she was the daughter of the Governor of Kovno, who had come for a visit.

The following night, with an audacity peculiar to Kiev collegians, he squeezed through the palisade into the garden and climbed a tree whose branches spread to the very roof of the house; from the tree he got on to the roof, and made his way down the chimney straight into the bedroom of the beautiful girl, who was at the moment sitting before a candlelight and removing her costly earrings from her ears. The beautiful girl was so alarmed on suddenly beholding a strange man that she was speechless; but when she perceived that the collegian stood with downcast eyes, too meek to move a finger, when she recognized that he was the boy that had tumbled down in the street before her eyes, she was again seized with laughter. Moreover, Andrei's features were not at all frightening—he was very handsome. So she laughed with all her heart and amused herself at his expense for a long time. The beautiful girl was as flighty as all Polish girls; but her eyes—her wonderful, clear and piercing eyes—darted

21

glances as long as time itself. The collegian stood stock-still, as though bound up in a sack, as the Governor's daughter boldly tripped up to him, put her sparkling tiara upon his head, hung her earrings on his lips, and draped him in a transparent muslin gown with gold-embroidered festoons. She dressed him up and played with him a thousand mischievous pranks, all with the childish abandon which marks the giddy Polish ladies, and which threw the poor collegian into still greater confusion. He cut a most ridiculous figure as he stood open-mouthed, staring into her dazzling eyes. A knock at the door startled her. She bade him crawl under the bed, and as soon as the coast was clear, she called her waiting-maid, a captive Tatar, and ordered her to conduct him quietly to the garden and thence to see him over the palisade. But this time Andrei was not so fortunate in clearing the fence; the watchman, awakening, smashed him over the legs, and the servants rushed out and beat him in the street for quite a long while until his swift legs took him to safety. After that it became very dangerous to pass the house, for the Governor's minions were numerous. He saw her once more in a Polish Roman Catholic church; she noticed him and gave him a bewitching smile, as to an old friend. He had another flitting glimpse of her, but shortly afterwards the Waywode of Kovno departed, and, instead of the fair dark-eyed Pole, a fat ugly face looked out of her windows.

This was what Andrei now kept pondering over, with hanging head and eyes fixed on his horse's mane.

In the meantime the steppe had long since received them all in its green embrace, and the tall grass, rising around them, had hidden them, till only their black Cossack caps appeared above it.

"Hey, there! Why so quiet, my lads?" cried Bulba, waking at last from his own reflections. "You're as glum as monks! Cast all your thoughts to the devil! Take your pipes in your teeth, light up, and let us spur on our horses and fly faster than any bird!"

And the Cossacks, spurring their horses, disappeared in the grass. Not even their black caps could now be seen, and only a streak of trampled grass marked their swift flight.

The sun had long since come out in the clear heavens and bathed the steppe in its warm, quickening light. All that was dim and dreamy fled at once from the Cossacks' minds; their hearts fluttered within them like birds.

The farther the steppe unrolled, the more beautiful it became. At that time all the South, as far as the Black Sea, all the land which is now Novorossia, was but one green, virgin wilderness. No plough had ever touched those boundless waves of wild growth.

Only horses trod down the tall grass, disappearing in it as in a forest. Nothing in Nature could be more beautiful. The earth's face looked like a green-gold ocean spouting millions of flowers. Through the tall, slender stems of the grass peeped blue, purple, and lilac cornflowers; the yellow broom shot high; the caps of the white clover dotted the plain; an ear of wheat, brought God knows from where, was ripening in the thicket. Among the slim stalks partridges pecked about with outstretched necks. The air was filled with the voices of a thousand different birds. In the sky hawks hung motionless with outspread wings, their eyes fixed immovably on the grass below. The cry of a cloud of wild geese, wheeling on one side of the horizon, was echoed from God knows what distant lake. From the grass a gull rose with measured stroke and bathed luxuriously in the blue currents of air. Behold, now it vanishes in the heights till only a black speck is visible, now it turns on the wing and gleams for an instant in the sunlight. O steppes, how beautiful you are!

Our travellers would halt but a few minutes for dinner, when their escort of ten Cossacks alighted, and untied the wooden casks of vodka and the pumpkins that served as cups. They ate only bread or wheaten biscuits with ham, drank but one cup apiece to fortify themselves, for Taras Bulba never allowed anyone to get drunk on the road, and then they would resume their journey until evening. In the evening a great change came over the steppe. All its many-hued expanse caught the sun's last flaming reflection and darkened gradually, so that the dusk could be seen closing over it, painting it dark-green; the vapours thickened: every flower, every herb breathed forth its scent, and the whole steppe was redolent. Broad bands of rosy gold, as if daubed on with a gigantic brush, stretched across the dark, blue tinted fields; here and there shreds of fluffy, transparent clouds gleamed whitely, and the freshest and most enchanting of breezes barely stirred the surface of the grass, gentle as sea waves, and softly touched the cheek. The music that had filled the day died away and gave place to another. The speckled gophers crept out of their holes, sat on their hind legs, and made the steppe resound with their whistle. The chirp of the grasshoppers became louder. A swan's cry was wafted, ringing silvery in the air, from some secluded lake.

The travellers would halt in the open field and choose a spot for their night camp; then they would make a fire, hang a cauldron over it, and cook their stew; the steam curled up in a slanting column. After supper the Cossacks turned their hobbled horses on to the grass and lay down to sleep, stretching themselves out on their cloaks. The stars looked down upon them. Their ears caught the teeming world of insects that filled the grass, their rasping, whistling, and chirping, which, magnified by the still air, rang clear and pure in the night and lulled the drowsy ear. If one of them happened to awake and arise, he saw the steppe spangled far and near with sparkling glow-worms. At times the night sky was illumined in spots by the distant glare of the dry reeds burning on the meadows and river-banks, and then, dark flights of swans, winging their way northwards, were suddenly lighted up by a silvery-pink gleam, and it seemed as if red kerchiefs were flying in the dark heavens.

The travellers rode on without any adventure. Not a single tree did they pass; it was ever the same endless steppe, free and beautiful. At rare intervals only did they spy the bluish summits of the far-away forest which bordered the bank of the Dnieper. Once only did Taras point to his sons a small dark speck in a distant field, saying, "Look, children, a Tatar rides yonder!" The little mustachioed face peered at them from afar with its small narrow eyes, sniffed the air hound-like, and vanished like an antelope, seeing the Cossacks were thirteen men. "Ho, lads! Would you overtake the Tatar? Better not try, you'd never catch him: his horse is swifter than my Devil." Yet, Bulba resorted to a subterfuge, fearing an ambush: they galloped to a small river, called the Tatarka, which flows into the Dnieper, sprang into the water, horses and all, and swam a long way to hide their trail; then they rode out on the bank and resumed their road.

Three days later they were near their destination. The air suddenly grew cooler: they felt the Dnieper was near. Now it sparkled afar and parted from the horizon in a dark band. It breathed chilly waves into the air and stretched near and nearer, till at last it covered half the land. Here the Dnieper, after being hemmed in by the rapids, finally gains the upper

24

hand, roaring like a sea and flowing far and wide; here the islands, flung into its midst, have forced it still farther out of its banks, and its waves, meeting neither crag nor hill, freely overflow the land. The Cossacks alighted from their horses, boarded a ferry-boat, and after a three hours' passage reached the shores of the island of Khortitsa, where the nomad Setch then lay.

A throng of people were squabbling on the shore with the ferrymen. Our Cossacks fastened the girths of their saddles. Taras assumed a dignified air, tightened his belt, and proudly stroked his moustache. His young sons, too, looked themselves over from head to heel, with a mingled feeling of vague anxiety and pleasurable anticipation. Then they all rode into a suburb that lay half a *verst* from the Setch. On entering it, they were deafened by fifty blacksmiths' hammers pounding in twenty-five smithies dug in the ground and thatched with turf. Strong-limbed curriers were squatting under porch-awnings in the street and kneading ox-hides with their sinewy hands. Tradesmen sat in their tents behind piles of flints and steels and gunpowder kegs. Here, an Armenian had hung out his costly kerchiefs; there, a Tatar was roasting spitted pieces of mutton rolled in dough. A Jew, his head thrust forward, was drawing vodka from a cask. But the first man they met was a Zaporozhian Cossack lying fast asleep in the very middle of the road, his legs and arms flung far apart. Taras Bulba could not help stopping to admire him.

"Phew, what a sight!" he cried, pulling up. "Ah, what a splendid manly figure he makes!"

And, in truth, the picture was a brave one: the Cossack stretched full length, like a lion, on the road; his hair, proudly thrown back, covered a full foot of ground. His wide trousers were smeared with tar—to proclaim his utter disdain for the rich scarlet cloth of which they were made.

Having admired the Cossack to his heart's content, Bulba rode into a narrow street crowded with craftsmen busy at their trades and with people of all nationalities thronging this Setch suburb, which resembled a fair and which clothed and fed the Setch, for the latter knew only how to shoot and carouse.

At last they left the suburb behind them and saw a few scattered Cossack huts, thatched with straw or, in Tatar fashion, with felt. Some were surrounded with cannon. Nowhere were there any fences or low-roofed houses with awnings propped by short wooden posts such as were seen in the suburb. A low stockaded rampart, totally unguarded, betokened a reckless lack of vigilance. A few sturdy Cossacks, who were lounging, pipe in mouth, in the middle of the road, glanced at them indifferently, but never bestirred themselves. Taras and his sons carefully picked their way among them, saying, "Good day, gentlemen!"—"And good day to you!" answered the Zaporozhians. The field was everywhere mottled with picturesque groups. Their swarthy faces bespoke them to be steeled in battle and tried in every sort of ordeal. So this was the Setch! Here was the lair of men proud and strong as lions! Hence poured freedom and Cossackdom over all the Ukraine!

The travellers rode into a great square, where the *Rada*, the general council of the Cossacks, usually assembled. A Zaporozhian was sitting there on a large overturned barrel; he had taken off his shirt and was slowly sewing up the holes in it. They were once again checked by a band of musicians, in whose midst a young Zaporozhian was dancing, his arms outstretched, his cap tilted at a devil-may-care angle. He was yelling again and again, "Play faster, musicians! And you, Foma, don't grudge these Christians their vodka!" And Foma, a Cossack with a black eye, meted out a large jugful to everyone who presented himself. Round the young Zaporozhian four old ones were tripping about quite briskly, now leaping aside like a whirlwind, almost upon the musicians' heads, then suddenly going into a gay squatting dance, vigorously drumming the hard earth with their silver-rimmed heels. The ground hummed far about, and the air resounded with the rhythms beaten out by the ringing hob-nailed boots. But there was one who yelled more lustily and flew about more quickly than all the rest. His hair tossed about in the wind, his muscular chest was quite bare; he had on a warm winter sheepskin coat, and the sweat was pouring down his body in buckets.

"Throw off your coat!" cried Taras at length. "You're steaming!"

"I can't," the Zaporozhian yelled back.

"Why?"

"I can't. I'm made that way: what I cast off buys me my vodka!"

26

And indeed, the fine young lad had no cap, no sash, no embroidered kerchief—all had gone the usual way.

The crowd was swelling; more people joined the dancers; and it was impossible for any onlooker not to be fired by the sight of the freest and wildest dance the world ever beheld, and which, from the name of its mighty inventors, is called the *kozachok*.

"I wish I weren't on horseback!" Taras exclaimed. "I'd join the dance myself!"

Among the throng, meanwhile, there began to appear staid old Cossacks, respected for their deeds by the whole Setch—who had more than once been chosen elders. Taras soon spied a host of familiar faces. Ostap and Andrei heard nothing but: "Ah, it is you, Pecheritsa! Good day, Kozolup!" —"Whence has God brought you, Taras?"—"How come you here, Doloto?"—"Hello, Kirdyaga! Hello, Gusty! Never thought I'd see you again, Remen!" And forthwith Taras exchanged kisses with these heroes, assembled from the wild steppes of eastern Russia; and then began to ask questions: "And what of Kasyan? Where is Borodavka? What of Kilopyor? How fares Pidsishok?" But all the answers Taras heard were that Borodavka had been hanged in Tolopan, that Kilopyor had been flayed alive near Kizikirmen, that Pidsishok's head had been salted and sent in a keg to Constantinople. Old Bulba hung his head and murmured thoughtfully, "Ah, but they were good Cossacks!"

CHAPTER THREE

TARAS BULBA and his sons had already spent about a week in the Setch. Ostap and Andrei occupied themselves but little with military training. The Setch did not like to trouble itself with military exercises and to waste its time on them; its youth was drilled and tempered by experience alone, in the heat of battles, of which, for that very reason, there was always enough. The Cossacks found it tiresome to fill up the intervals with the study of any warlike art, except perhaps marksmanship and, on rare occasions, horse-racing and wild-beast chasing in the meadows and steppes; the rest of their time was spent in making merry—a sign of the untrammelled breadth of their souls.

The Setch presented an unusual scene, one of unbroken revelry, a festival noisily begun and with no end in sight. Some busied themselves with their crafts; others kept stalls and traded; but the greater part caroused from morning till night—if the wherewithal still jingled in their pockets and their loot had not yet passed into the hands of tradesmen and pot-house keepers. There was something exhilarating about this universal festival. It was no gathering of revellers drowning their sorrow in wine, but simply a riotous outburst of merrymaking. Every man who came thither forgot and cast behind him all his troubles. He spat on all his past, in a manner of speaking, and plunged recklessly into free living in the company of men, who, roisterers like himself, had neither home nor family, nought but the open heavens and the eternal revel of their souls. This bred that fierce gaiety that could never have sprung from any other source. The tales that spread through the crowds of Cossacks lazily reposing on the ground were often so mirth-provoking and vivid that it took all a Zaporozhian's outward composure to keep a straight face, without even a twitch of the moustache —a striking feature which to this day distinguishes the Southern Russians from the rest of their brethren. Drunken, boisterous jollity it was; and yet it was no gloomy pot-house where a man loses himself in counterfeited hideous gaiety; here was a close-knit band of school-mates. The sole difference was that instead of following their tutor's pointer and listening to his silly lessons, they would mount five thousand horses and go off on a raid; that instead of the field where they played ball, they had their recklessly unguarded frontiers where the swift Tatar showed his head and the green-turbaned Turk stared grimly. The difference was that instead of the coercive will which had brought them together at school, they themselves had run away from their parental homes, had left their fathers and mothers; here were those who had already felt the noose tightening around their necks, and who, instead of that bloodless death, had seen life —life in all its riotousness; here were those who, according to the noble custom, could never retain a single kopek in their pockets; here were those who had regarded a ducat as wealth, and whose pockets, thanks to the revenue-farmers, could always be turned inside out without fear of dropping anything. Here were those collegians who had not been able to put up with the academic rod, and had not carried away a single letter of the alphabet from school. But besides them there were those here who knew about Horace, Cicero, and the Roman Republic. Here were many officers who later distinguished themselves under the colors of the King of Poland, and a great many seasoned partisans whose noble conviction it was that it mattered not where they fought so long as they did fight, as it did not behoove an honorable man to live without fighting. Many were here, too, who had come to the Setch merely to be able to say afterwards that they had been at the Setch and were already hardened knights. But who was not here? This strange republic was a child of the epoch. Lovers of war, golden goblets, rich brocades, diamonds and pieces of eight could at all times find employment here. Those only who worshipped women could find nothing to do here, for no woman dared show herself even in the suburb of the Setch.

To Ostap and Andrei it seemed exceedingly strange that a great crowd of people had entered the Setch with them and no one had asked them whence they came, who they were, and what were their names. They came there as if returning to a home left only an hour before. The newcomer presented himself only to the *Koshevoi Ataman*, who usually said:

"Welcome, good fellow! Do you believe in Christ?"

"I do," replied the newcomer.

"And do you believe in the Holy Trinity?"

"I do!"

"And do you go to church?"

"Yes."

"Let's see you cross yourself."

The newcomer made the sign of the cross.

"All right," said the *Koshevoi*. "Go and choose any hut you like."

This ended the ceremony.

The whole Setch prayed in one church and was ready to defend it to the last drop of blood, although it would not even hear of fasting or temperance. Only the most covetous of Armenians and Tatars dared to live and trade in the suburb, because the Zaporozhians never bargained and threw down as much money as their hand happened to take out of their pocket. But the fate of these grasping traders was miserable in the extreme. They were like the people who settled at the foot of Mount Vesuvius, for as soon as the Zaporozhians had squandered their money, these desperadoes smashed their stalls and took what they wanted gratis.

The Setch consisted of sixty barracks, each of which resembled a separate, independent republic, and bore an even greater resemblance to a boarding school. No one thought of starting a house or acquiring possessions. Everything was in the hands of the *ataman* (chief) of the *kuren*, who was consequently called *Batko* (Father); he had charge of funds and clothes, of all the food down to porridge and flour gruel, and even of the firewood. They gave him their money to take care of. Quite often the *kurens* quarrelled with one another. In such cases they at once passed from words to blows. The *kurens* covered the square and curried each other's carcasses until one of them gained the upper hand, and then they all joined in a binge. This was the Setch, which had so many attractions for young men.

Ostap and Andrei threw themselves with all the ardor of youth into this ocean of revelry, promptly forgetting their father's house, the Academy, and all that had hitherto filled their minds, and gave themselves up to their new life. Everything here interested them—the riotous habis of the Setch, its simple administration and its laws, which at times seemed inordinately severe in so free a republic. A Cossack found guilty of theft, no matter how petty, was considered a disgrace to all Cossackdom; the ignoble wretch was tied to the "post of shame" and a club was laid beside him, with which every passer-by was bound to deal him a blow until in this manner he was clubbed to death. A Cossack who would not pay his debts was chained to a cannon, and there he remained till one of his comrades ransomed him by paying his debts. But nothing impressed Andrei so much as the terrible punishment decreed for murder. Before his very eyes a hole was dug, the murderer was thrown into it alive, and a coffin with the body of his victim was placed over him; and both were buried. For a long time afterwards Andrei was haunted by the memory of the horrible execution and the man buried alive together with the terrible coffin.

Soon both youths were in very good standing with the Cossacks. They often rode out into the steppe with comrades of their own *kuren*, or sometimes even with the whole *kuren* in full strength together with neighbouring *kurens*, to shoot an innumerable quantity of steppe birds of every sort, as well as deer and goats, or else they would go to lakes, rivers and river branches, assigned to every *kuren* by lot, cast their sweep-nets and land rich hauls to replenish their *kuren's* food stock. Though there was nothing in all this to test them as Cossacks, they soon won distinction among the other youths by their daring and luck in everything. They were bold and sure marksmen, and could swim across the Dnieper against the current—an exploit for which they were triumphantly admitted into Cossack circles.

But old Taras had in mind other exploits for them. His nature revolted at the idle life they were leading and thirsted for real action. He kept thinking how he could raise the Setch on a brave venture calling for knightly prowess. At length he went one day to the *Koshevoi* and asked him point-blank, "Well, *Koshevoi*, isn't it high time we Zaporozhians took the field?"

"There's nowhere to go," answered the *Koshevoi*, taking his short pipe from his mouth and spitting aside.

"Nowhere to go! We can go against the Tatars or against the Turks."

"We can't go either against the Turks or the Tatars," answered the *Koshevoi*, coolly putting his pipe into his mouth again.

"Why can't we?"

"We have promised peace to the Sultan."

"But he is an unbeliever; and God and Holy Writ command us to punish all unbelievers."

"We've no right to. If we had not sworn by our faith, we might have done it, but now—no, we can't."

"Why can't we? What do you mean by saying we have no right to? Here am I with two sons, both of them young men. Neither of them has been to war, and you say we've no right. Do you mean to say the Zaporozhians can't go to war?"

"Well, that's the way it must be."

"Must Cossack strength, then, be wasted in vain? Must a man die like a dog without having done any worthy deed, without any use to his country or Christendom? What, then, do we live for? Tell me, what the devil do we live for? You are a clever man; you weren't elected *Koshevoi* for nothing, so just tell me what we live for?"

The *Koshevoi* made no reply to this question. He was an obstinate Cossack. He remained silent for a while, and then said, "All the same, there will be no war."

"There will be no war, you say?" Taras asked again.

"No."

"And it's no use thinking about it?"

"No use."

"Wait, you devil's son!" said Bulba to himself. "I'll show you!" And he forthwith resolved to take his revenge on the *Koshevoi*.

After having talked with a number of comrades, he treated them all to plenty of liquor, and soon the drunk Cossacks made in a body for the square, where, tied to a post, stood the kettle-drum, which was generally used for summoning the *Rada*. Not finding the sticks, as the drummer always kept them on his person, they each seized a log of wood and began beating the drum. The first to respond to the drum-beat was the drummer himself, a tall man who managed to look frightfully sleepy-eyed although he had but one eye.

"Who dares beat the drum?" he shouted.

"Silence! Take your sticks and beat the drum when you are ordered," replied the tipsy elders.

The drummer, knowing only too well how such incidents ended, at once took from his pocket the sticks. The kettle-drum boomed, and soon the Zaporozhians came swarming up like black bumble-bees. They all assembled in a ring, and at length, after the third summons, the chiefs appeared: the *Koshevoi* with the mace, the token of his office; the judge with the army seal; the scrivener with his ink-horn; and the *esaul* with his staff. The *Koshevoi* and the other chiefs doffed their caps and bowed low on all sides to the Cossacks, who stood there proudly with their arms akimbo.

"What means this assembly? What is your wish, gentlemen?" asked the *Koshevoi*.

Shouts and curses silenced him.

"Put down the mace! Lay it down at once, devil's son! We don't want you any longer!" roared the Cossacks from the crowd. Some of the sober *kurens* seemed inclined to disagree; at length the *kurens*, sober and otherwise, came to blows. The yells and uproar became universal.

The *Koshevoi* tried to speak, but then thought better of it; knowing that the infuriated, self-willed crowd might beat him to death, as almost always happened on such occasions, he bowed very low, laid down the mace, and vanished in the crowd.

"Do you, gentlemen, command us to lay down the tokens of our rank, too?" said the judge, the scrivener, and the *esaul*, making ready to resign ink-horn, army seal, and staff.

"No, carry on!" the crowd shouted. "We only wanted to get rid of the *Koshevoi* because he's nothing but an old woman, and we need a man for *Koshevoi*."

"Whom do you now choose as *Koshevoi*?"

"Choose Kukubenko!" shouted one side.

"We don't want Kukubenko!" shouted the other. "He's too young; his mother's milk is still on his lips!"

"Let Shilo be the Ataman!" shouted some. "Choose Shilo as *Koshevoi!*"

"Too much foolishness in Shilo!" the crowd yelled and swore. "What kind of Cossack is he when he is as thieving as a Tatar, the hound's son! To hell with the drunkard Shilo! Brain him with a shillalah!"

"Borodaty! Let's make Borodaty our *Koshevoi!*"

"We don't want Borodaty! A curse upon the bastard!"

"Shout for Kirdyaga!" Taras Bulba whispered to some.

"Kirdyaga! Kirdyaga!" screamed the crowd.

"Borodaty! Borodaty!"

"Kirdyaga! Kirdyaga!"

"Shilo!"

"To the devil with Shilo!"

"Kirdyaga!"

All the candidates instantly stepped out of the crowd as soon as they heard their names shouted, lest anyone should think they had personally influenced their election.

"Kirdyaga! Kirdyaga!" was heard ever louder.

"Borodaty!"

They began to settle the dispute by a violent display of fists, and Kirdyaga triumphed.

"Go and fetch Kirdyaga!"

About a dozen Cossacks detached from the crowd—some of them could scarcely manage to keep their feet, so overloaded they were with vodka—and marched directly to Kirdyaga to tell him of his election.

Kirdyaga, a rather old but clever Cossack, had been sitting in his *kuren* for quite a long time, as if he knew nothing of the goings on.

"What do you want, gentlemen?" he asked.

"Come; you have been chosen *Koshevoi.*"

"Have mercy, gentlemen!" said Kirdyaga. "I am the last man to be worthy of such an honor. A fine *Koshevoi* I should make! I have not sense enough for such a post. Could they not find a better man in the whole army?"

"Come on, I tell you!" the Zaporozhians shouted.

Two of them grasped him by the arms, and though he balked and jibed, he was dragged to the square, goaded on by blows and kicks, swearing and exhortations: "Don't hang back, you devil's son! Take the honour, dog, when it is given to you."

34

In this manner Kirdyaga was conducted into the circle of Cossacks.

"Well, gentlemen," his escort bellowed to the crowd, "do you all agree to have this Cossack for your *Koshevoi?*"

"We agree!" roared the crowd; and the plain resounded long with the roar.

One of the chiefs took up the mace and offered it to the newly-elected *Koshevoi*. Kirdyaga, as custom demanded, refused it. The chief offered it a second time. Kirdyaga refused it again, and only after the third invitation did he take the mace. A yell of approval rose from the crowd, and it was re-echoed by the whole plain. Then from the midst of the crowd there stepped the four oldest Cossacks, whitewhiskered and with white scalp-locks (no very old folk were to be found in the Setch, for no Zaporozhian ever died a natural death); each picked up a handful of earth—which recent rain had turned into mud—and placed it on Kirdyaga's head. The mud trickled down his head to his moustache and cheeks, smearing his whole face. But Kirdyaga stood unflinchingly and thanked the Cossacks for the honour they had done him.

So ended that noisy election; it remains unknown whether anyone rejoiced in its outcome as much as Bulba: he had taken his revenge on the former *Koshevoi;* moreover, Kirdyaga was an old comrade of his, who had been with him in the same campaigns, over sea and land, sharing with him the toils and rigours of a soldier's life. The crowd at once scattered to celebrate the election, and a riot began such as Ostap and Andrei had never seen before. The pot-houses were ransacked; meads, vodka, and beer were carried off without payment; the keepers were glad to escape with their lives. The whole night through they shouted and sang martial songs. The rising moon gazed down on bands of musicians walking about the streets with banduras, tambourines, round balalaikas, and choristers who were kept in the Setch to chant in church and to glorify the deeds of the Zaporozhians. At last, drink and fatigue began to get the better of these strong heads. Here and there a Cossack could be seen falling to the ground. Here a Cossack hugged a comrade until, growing maudlin and even bursting into tears, they both collapsed. There a whole group lay in a heap; there a man looked about for the best place to sleep and stretched

35

himself out in a trough. The toughest Cossack of all still mumbled incoherently; finally even he, too, was overpowered by intoxication; he toppled down—and all the Setch slept.

CHAPTER FOUR

NEXT DAY Taras Bulba was already discussing with the new *Koshevoi* the best way of committing the Zaporozhians to action. The *Koshevoi*, a clever cunning Cossack, knew the Zaporozhians thoroughly, and began by saying, "We can't break our oath, not on any account." Then, after a pause, he added, "But there is a way; we will not break our oath, but we might think of something. Just have the people assemble, not at my order, but of their own free will. You know best how to manage that. And the chiefs and I will run to the square as if we knew nothing about it."

In less than an hour after their conversation the drums were rolling. The Cossacks, however tipsy and befuddled, assembled at once. A million Cossack caps were all at once bobbing in the square. A murmur arose, "Who . . ." What for . . . ? Why this muster?" No one answered them. At length, in one quarter and in another, disgruntled voices were raised, "Our Cossack strength is being wasted: there is no war! The chiefs are grown lazy; their eyes are bloated with fat! There's no justice in the world!" The other Cossacks listened at first, and then themselves began to complain, "Aye, in very truth, there is no justice in the world!" The chiefs professed astonishment at these words. At last the

Koshevoi stepped forward and said, "Permit me, gentlemen Zaporozhians, to make a speech."

"Out with it!"

"The purport of my speech, most virtuous gentlemen, is to tell you . . . but perchance you know it better than I do . . . that many Zaporozhians have run into such debt to the pot-houses and to their own brethren that no devil will give them any credit. Furthermore, the purport of my speech is to tell you that there are many young blades who have not the faintest idea of what war is like, whereas you know, gentlemen, that no young man can live without war. What manner of Zaporozhian is he if he never beat an infidel?"

"He speaks well," thought Bulba.

"But think not, gentlemen, that I speak thus to break the peace; God forbid! I merely state the facts. Besides, look at what sort of God's temple we have here; it's a disgrace to us: the Setch, by the mercy of God, has stood for years and years, but to this day, not to say anything of the outer appearance of our church, the images inside are without any trappings. No one has thought even of forging at least a silver frame for them! Our church has received but what some Cossacks have left it in their wills. Yea, and these gifts were poor, because the givers had drunk up nearly all their belongings in their lifetime. But the purport of my speech is not to tell you to make war against the infidels; we have promised the Sultan peace, and we should take a great sin upon our souls, for we have sworn by our faith."

"What is the meaning of all that trash?" Bulba wondered.

"So you see, gentlemen, that we can't begin war. Our knightly honour does not permit it. But my silly old head makes me think that we might send out our young men in boats, and let them "scrape" the coasts of Anatolia a little. What do you say to that, gentlemen?"

"Lead us, lead us all!" shouted the crowd on all sides.

"We are ready to lay down our heads for our faith!" The *Koshevoi* was alarmed; he had not at all meant to raise the whole of Zaporozhye; he thought it unfair to violate the peace on this occasion.

"Permit me, gentlemen, to make another speech."

"Enough!" yelled the Zaporozhians. "Don't spoil the first one."

"If you will have it so, so let it be. I am but the slave of your will. Everyone knows, and the Holy Writ says so, that the voice of the people is the voice of God. No counsel is better than the counsel of the whole people. But I was thinking of this: you know, gentlemen, that the Sultan would not let the pleasant little adventure of our young men go unpunished. And meanwhile we should be ready for him, and our forces should be fresh, and we should have no cause to fear anyone. Besides, the Tatars may come down on the Setch when we are away; those Turkish dogs will never dare to come while the master is at home; but they will bite our heels from behind, and bite painfully, too. If the whole truth must be told, we have not enough boats in store, nor has there been ground enough gunpowder, for all to set out. As for myself, I'm for it, for I am but the slave of your will."

The cunning Ataman fell silent. The crowd broke up into groups and began to discuss the matter; the *kuren* chiefs put their heads together. It was resolved to follow the prudent advice.

A number of men were at once dispatched to the opposite bank of the Dnieper, to the treasury of the army, where the army treasure and part of the arms captured from the enemy lay concealed in hiding-places under water and among the reeds. All the others rushed to the boats, to inspect and prepare them for the expedition. In a twinkling the whole shore was covered with people. Carpenters appeared, axe in hand. Sunburnt, broad-shouldered, sturdy-legged elderly Zaporozhians, with black and greying moustaches, stood knee-deep in the water, their trousers rolled up, and pulled at the stout ropes, dragging the boats into the water. Others were hauling dry logs and newly-felled trees. Here they were planking a boat; there a boat, turned bottom upwards, was being caulked and tarred; there long bundles of reeds were being fastened to the boats, after the Cossack fashion, that they might not be washed over by the sea waves; all along the shore fires were built and tar was being boiled in copper cauldrons for tarring the boats. The old and experienced instructed the young. The noise and shouts of work arose on all sides; the shore itself seemed to come alive with the stir and movement.

Just then a large ferry-boat was nearing the shore. The crowd of people in it had already at a distance begun to wave their hands. They were Cossacks in ragged, miserable garments—some, indeed, had on nothing but their shirts and a short pipe in their mouths—which showed that they had either just escaped from some disaster or had feasted away all they had off their backs. From among them came forward a short, thickset, broad-shouldered Cossack of about fifty. He yelled louder and waved his hand more vigorously than any; but his words were drowned by the noise and shouts of the workmen.

"What tidings do you bring?" asked the *Koshevoi*, when the ferry made fast at the shore.

All the workmen, pausing in their labours with raised axe and chisel, looked on in expectation.

"Evil tidings!" shouted the thickset Cossack from the ferry-boat.

"What are they?"

"Do you permit me, gentlemen Zaporozhians, to make a speech?"

"Speak out!"

"Or perchance you will call a *Rada?*"

"Speak, we are all here." The people crowded together.

"Have you not heard of the goings on in the hetmanship?"

"And what is going on there?" asked one of the kuren atamans.

"What! It seems the Tatars have wadded up your ears that you heard nothing."

"Well, tell us what is doing there."

"Such things are doing there as no born and baptized man has ever seen before."

"Tell us what's doing there, you son of a dog!" yelled one of the crowd, losing patience.

"Such times are come upon us that even our holy churches are not our own."

"How not our own?"

"They have been leased to the Jews. If the Jew is not paid in advance, there can be no service."

"The man must be raving!"

"And if the damned dog of a Jew does not put his mark on our holy Easter-bread with his unclean hands, it cannot be consecrated."

"He lies, gentlemen brothers! It cannot be that an unclean Jew puts his mark upon the holy Easter-bread!"

"Listen! That's not all. Roman priests are riding about all over the Ukraine in carriages. But the trouble lies not in the carriages, the trouble is that they harness not horses any longer, but Orthodox Christians. Listen! That's not all: they say that the Jewesses are already making themselves petticoats out of our priests' vestments. That, gentlemen, is what is doing in the Ukraine! And you sit here in Zaporozhye carousing, and the Tatars, it seems, have so frightened you that you have no eyes, no ears, no anything, and you know nothing of what is doing in the world."

"Wait, wait!" broke in the Koshevoi, who up till then had stood with his eyes fixed upon the ground like all Zaporozhians, who in a grave situation never yielded to their first impulse, but kept their own counsel and quietly worked up themselves to the pitch of indignation. "Wait! Tell me this: what were *you* doing—may your fathers be drawn and quartered by the devil—what were you doing yourselves? Had you no swords? How came you to permit such lawlessness?"

"How came we? Would you have stopped them when there were fifty thousand Poles and when—it's no use to conceal our sins!—there were dogs among our own folk who have already accepted their faith?"

"And your chiefs and colonels—where were they?"

"God preserve us from the fate of our colonels!"

"How so?"

"Our chief now lies roasted in a copper pot in Warsaw; and the heads and hands of our colonels are being carted from fair to fair for all the people to see. Such is the fate of our colonels!"

The whole crowd came to life. At first a hush fell over the shore, as before a fierce storm; then all at once voices were raised and all the shore burst into speech.

"What! Jews renting Christian churches! Roman priests harnessing Orthodox Christians to their carriages! What! To permit such torments to be suffered on Russian soil because of the accursed Papists! To let them so treat our colonels and our chiefs! No, this must not, this shall not be!"

Such words ran through every part of the crowd.

The Zaporozhians gave vent to their fury; they became conscious of their strength. It was no longer the excitement of a light-minded people; this was the excitement of strong and firm characters, which, though not easily fired, burned long and stubbornly.

Everyone had at once left the shore and the boats, for now it was to be not a sea expedition, but a land campaign, so that they needed horses and wagons, not ships and skiffs. Young

41

and old, all now wanted to take part in the campaign; all resolved, on the advice of the elders, the kuren atamans, and the Koshevoi, and by the unanimous assent of all the Zaporozhian army, to march straight into Poland, avenge the injury and disgrace to their faith and to Cossack glory; to loot every town, set fire to the villages and the fields; and to spread their fame far and wide over the steppe. All at once girded and armed themselves. The Koshevoi seemed to grow a whole head taller. He was no longer the meek executor of a lawless people's giddy whims, but their absolute lord. He was a despot, who knew but to command. All these self-willed and pleasure-seeking knights stood arrayed in orderly ranks, with heads bowed respectfully, not daring to raise their eyes, while the Koshevoi gave his orders; he gave them quietly, without any noise or haste, weighing his words as became an old and seasoned Cossack veteran, who had led many a cleverly planned enterprise.

"Look carefully, look carefully to everything," so he spoke. "Look to your wagons and your tar-pails, and test your weapons. Do not take too much clothing with you: a shirt and two pairs of trousers each, and a pot of flour and another of ground millet—let no man take any more. There will be plenty of everything in the wagons. Every Cossack should have two horses. And we must have about two hundred yoke of oxen, for we shall need them for the fords and bogs. Above all, gentlemen, keep order. There are some among you, I know, who, when God puts booty in their way, fall to tearing up costly velvet for foot-wraps. Renounce that devilish habit; drop the petticoats and take only weapons, if they be good ones, and silver, for they are capacious things and are certain to come in handy. And this I tell you beforehand that if anyone gets drunk upon the road, he will have a short shrift. I will have him tied by the neck, like a dog, to a wagon, whoever he be, were he even the army's most valiant Cossack. I will have him shot on the spot like a dog and left without burial to be torn by the vultures, for a drunkard on the march does not deserve Christian burial. You, young men, must obey your elders in all things. If you are nipped by a bullet or scratched by a sword—head or any other part—think little of it. Just mix a charge of gunpowder in a cup of vodka, swallow it at a draught, and all will be well—neither will you have any fever; and on the wound, if it be not too large, simply put some earth, mixing it first with spittle in the palm of the hand, and the wound will dry up. Well, now to business, lads, and let there be no needless hurry, and do everything well!"

So spoke the Koshevoi; and then all the Cossacks set about their business. All the Setch had at once grown sober; nowhere was a single drunken man to be found, as though there never had been any drunks among the Cossacks.

Some repaired the wheels and changed the axles of the wagons; others loaded them with sacks of provisions and with arms; still others drove in the horses and oxen. On all sides was heard the thud of horses' hoofs; the test firing of guns; the rattle of swords; the lowing of oxen; the creaking of wagons driven out on to the road; the voices and ringing shouts of the Cossacks; the urging-on of the drivers. Presently the Cossack cavalcade stretched out across the plain; and he who would run from its van to its rear would have a long trip before him.

In the small wooden church the priest held a farewell service, and sprinkled one and all with holy water; all kissed the cross. When the cavalcade set out and was leaving the Setch, all the Zaporozhians turned their heads back.

"Farewell, our Mother!" they said almost in one breath. "May God preserve you from all misfortune!"

CHAPTER FIVE

SOON ALL south-western Poland became a prey to fear. Everywhere the rumor had passed, "The Zaporozhians! The Zaporozhians are coming!" All who could save themselves by flight, fled. All rose and scattered after the manner of that orderless, careless time, when neither fortresses nor castles were erected, but man knocked together a makeshift straw hut, thinking, "What is the use of spending money and labor on a good house, when a Tatar raid will raze it anyway!" All were on the run: one exchanged his plough and oxen for a horse and gun and joined his regiment; another went into hiding, driving off his cattle and carrying away all that could be carried. Some rose up in arms to meet the strangers; but the majority fled before them. All knew that it was hard to fight the violent and warlike horde known by the name of the Zaporozhian army, which under a self-willed, disorderly exterior concealed discipline exceedingly well-fitted for warfare. The mounted Cossacks took care not to overburden or heat their horses; the rest walked soberly behind their wagons; the whole force moved only by night, spending the day in wild, uninhabited fields and in forests, of which at that time there were many. Spies and scouts were sent ahead to ascertain the where, what, and how of the enemy. And often the Zaporozhians suddenly turned up where they were least expected, leaving nothing but death in their wake. They set fire to the villages; the cattle and horses were either driven off by the army or slaughtered on the spot. It was more like a bloody feast than a military expedition. One would be shocked today at the sight of the horrible trail of atrocities—a sight common enough in that half-savage age—left by the Zaporozhians wherever they set foot. Murdered children, women's breasts cut away, the skin torn from the legs of those who were set free—yes, the Cossacks were paying their debts in full.

The abbot of one monastery, hearing of their approach, sent two monks to the Cossacks to tell them that they were misbehaving; that the Zaporozhians and the government were at peace; that they were not only violating their duty to their king, but common law as well.

"Tell the bishop from me and from all the Zaporozhians," said the Koshevoi, "that he has nothing to fear. The Cossacks are merely making fire to light their pipes."

And soon after, the magnificent abbey was hugged by a devastating blaze, and its great Gothic windows looked grimly through the surging billows of fire.

Crowds of refugees—monks, Jews, and women—filled to overflowing those towns whose garrisons and militia could be hoped to offer them protection. At times the government belatedly sent help in the form of a few troops; but these either failed to find the Zaporozhians or were seized with panic and turned tail at the first encounter, fleeing on their swift horses. It happened that quite a few of the king's captains, who had won glory in former battles, resolved to unite their forces and make a firm stand against the Zaporozhians.

Then it was that our young Cossacks—despising pillage, looting, and a feeble foe, but burning with the desire to show their worth to their leaders really put their prowess to the trial by entering into single combat with the dashing and boastful Pole, who cut a splendid figure on his proud steed, the loose sleeves of his cloak streaming in the wind. Learning the art of war was like a game to the young Cossacks. They had already won a great many horse-trappings and valuable sabres and muskets. In a month these tyros had become warriors; they had become men. Their features, which hitherto had worn a youthful softness, were now grim and strong. Old Taras was overjoyed to see both his sons take their place among the foremost. Ostap seemed born to tread the path of war, to scale the summits of its difficult art. Never faltering or flinching under any circumstances, with a coolness almost unnatural in a man of twenty-two, he could instantly measure the perils of any impasse and at once devise a way of escaping it, so that he might the more surely triumph in the end. His every action was now marked by the assurance born of experience, and in all he did was clearly to be seen the promise of a future leader. His body breathed forth strength; his knightly qualities had already burgeoned into mighty and leonine qualities.

"Ah, but he will make a good colonel yet," old Taras would say. "Yea, he will even outshine his own Batko."

The music of blades and bullets held Andrei in its spell. He knew not what it is to consider, calculate, or gauge beforehand his own and his adversary's strength. He was blinded by the fierce joy and ecstasy of battle; to him there was something festive in those moments when a man's brain is on fire —when everything whirls and swims before his eyes—when heads fly—when horses crash down, and he gallops, like a man drunk with wine, amidst the whistling of balls and the flashing of sabres, and cuts right and left, and never feels the blows showering on himself. Many were the times when his father marvelled, too, at Andrei, seeing him fling himself, driven on by sheer love of battle, into dangers a cool and sensible man would never have risked and, by the sheer audacity of his mad onslaught, perform such wonders as could not but amaze warriors grown old in battle. Old Taras marvelled at him, and said, "He, too, is a good soldier—God preserve him! Not as good as Ostap, but still a good soldier!"

The army resolved to march straight on the town of Dubno, where, rumor had it, there were rich coffers and wealthy townsfolk. In a day and a half the march was accomplished, and the Zaporozhians appeared before the city. The inhabitants were determined to defend themselves to the last, and to die in the squares and streets, and on their thresholds, rather than let the enemy into their houses. High earthen ramparts surrounded the town; where they were low there projected a stone wall, or a house serving as a redoubt, or at least an oaken stockade. The garrison was strong and aware of the importance of its duty. The Zaporozhians tried to storm the ramparts but were met by a hail of grapeshot. The burghers and townsfolk evidently did not wish to remain idle, for they stood in a crowd on the ramparts. Their eyes promised desperate resistance. The women likewise had decided to bear a hand in the defense; and upon the heads of the Zaporozhians rained stones, barrels, pots, and hot pitch, and sackfuls of sand which blinded them. The Zaporozhians disliked having to deal with fortresses: sieges were not their field.

The Koshevoi ordered them to fall back and said, "Never mind, gentlemen brothers, we will retreat. But may I be a heathen Tatar, and not a Christian, if we let any one of them out of the town. Let the dogs all perish of hunger!"

The army retreated, surrounded the town, and, for lack of anything better to do, busied itself with laying waste the surrounding country, burning the neighboring villages and ricks of wheat in the fields and turning herds of horses to graze in the cornfields, as yet untouched by the scythe, where nodded, as if in mockery, the heavy ears of wheat, the fruit of a wondrous rich harvest which that season was the generous reward of all farmers. The town was terror-struck to see their means of subsistence being destroyed. Meanwhile the Zaporozhians, having strung out their wagons in a double ring around the town, camped as in the Setch in kurens, sucked their pipes, exchanged prize weapons, played at leapfrog and odd-and-even, and glanced with killing calm at the town. Watchfires were lighted at night. In every kuren the cooks boiled gruel in huge copper cauldrons. Alert sentinels stood beside the fires, which burnt all night.

But the Zaporozhians soon began to tire of inactivity and of protracted sobriety unaccompanied by any fighting. The Koshevoi even ordered the wine allowance to be doubled, which was sometimes done in the army when there were no hard feats or marches on hand. This life was not to the liking of the young Cossacks, especially the sons of Taras Bulba. Andrei was plainly bored.

"You hothead!" said Taras to him. "Bear all, Cossack, and ye'll be chief yet! He is not a good warrior who does not lose heart in the fiercest battle, but he who can stand even idleness, who endures all and has his own way whatever the odds."

But youth and old age never agree. The two are of different natures, and they look with different eyes at the same thing.

In the meantime Bulba's regiment, led by Tovkach, caught

up with the army; with him were two more esauls, the scrivener, and the other regimental officers. In all, the Cossacks mustered four thousand strong. Among them were a good many mounted men, who had risen of their own free will, without any summons, as soon as they heard what was afoot.

To each of Bulba's sons the esauls brought their old mother's blessing and a cypress icon from the Mezhigorsk Monastery in Kiev. Both brothers hung the holy images round their necks, and despite themselves grew pensive at the thought of their old mother. What did her blessing mean, what did it forebode? Was it a blessing for their victory over the enemy, and then for a happy return to the land of their fathers, with booty and glory, ever to be sung by the bandura-players? Or was it . . . ? But the future is unknown, and it stands before man like the autumn mist that rises over the marsh; birds fly blindly up and down in it, flapping their wings and never seeing each other—the hawk seeing not the dove, nor the dove the hawk—and none ever knowing how far he may be flying from his death. . . .

Ostap had long since returned to his duties and gone to the kurens. But Andrei, though he knew not why, felt a stifling weight at his heart. Already the Cossacks had finished their supper; evening had long since faded; the beautiful July night had filled the air; still he did not go to the kurens, nor lie down to sleep, captivated by the picture before him. Numberless stars twinkled, clear-cut and sharp, in the sky. The field was strewn far and wide with wagons, loaded with various goods and provisions captured from the enemy, with dripping tar-buckets hanging under them. All about the wagons Zaporozhians were to be seen, sprawling on the grass. They slept in peculiar positions, their heads resting on a sack, or a cap, or simply on a comrade's side. Sword, pistol, short-stemmed pipe with brass mountings, wire brushes and flint-box were inseparable from every Cossack. The heavy bullocks lay like huge whitish masses, their feet turned under them, resemblin grey boulders scattered on the slopes of the field. On all sides the sonorous snoring of the sleeping host had already begun to arise, and was answered from the field by the ringing neigh of the stallions, indignant at having their feet hobbled. Meanwhile the beauty of the July night had acquired a magnificent and awesome quality. It was the glare of the neighboring districts which had not yet burned to the ground. In one place the flame spread slowly and majesti-

48

cally over the heaven; in another, meeting with something inflammable and bursting into a whirlwind, it hissed and flew upwards to the very stars, and its severed tongues died in the highest regions of the sky. Here stood the charred, black monastery, like a stern Carthusian monk, displaying its gloomy grandeur at every new outburst of flame; there blazed the monastery garden. One could almost hear the trees hissing as they were wrapped up in smoke; and as the fire broke through, it suddenly lighted up clusters of ripe plums with a hot phosphorescent, violet gleam or turned the yellow pears here and there to pure gold; and in the midst of all this, hanging against the wall of the building or from a bough, would be seen the black figure of some poor Jew or monk whom the fire was devouring together with the building. Birds, hovering far away above the conflagration, looked like a mass of tiny black crosses upon a fiery field. The beleaguered town seemed to be slumbering. Its spires, roofs, stockade, and walls flickered quietly in the glare of the distant conflagrations.

Andrei walked around the rows of Cossack wagons. The watch-fires were about to die out at any moment, and the sentries themselves were fast asleep, having stuffed themselves with flour gruel and galushki with true Cossack appetite. Somewhat surprised at such carelessness, he thought, "It is well that there is no strong foe at hand, no one to fear." At last, he went to one of the wagons, climbed into it, and lay down upon his back, folding his hands under his head; but he could not sleep and gazed long at the sky. It was all open before him: the air was pure and limpid. The thicket of stars forming the Milky Way and girding the heavens was flooded with light. From time to time Andrei fell into a drowse; a light mist of slumber veiled the sky before him for a spell; then it cleared and again became visible.

It was at such a moment that a strange human face seemed to flit before his eyes. Thinking it to be but an illusion of sleep which would at once vanish, he opened his eyes wider and saw that a withered, emaciated face was actually bent over him, its eyes looking into his. Long coal-black hair, unkempt, dishevelled, hung from beneath a dark veil thrown over the head. The strange glint in the eyes and the deathlike swarthiness of the sharp-featured face could surely belong to none but a phantom. Involuntarily he reached for his pistol and asked almost convulsively, "Who are you? If an evil

49

spirit, be gone; if human and alive, your jest is ill-timed. Go, or I will kill you with one shot."

In answer to this, the spectre put its finger on his lips and seemed to entreat silence. He lowered his hand and looked at the apparition more closely. From the long hair, the neck, and the half-naked bosom, he recognized it to be a woman. But she was not a native of these parts. Her washed face was swarthy; her wide cheek-bones protruded sharply over her shrunken cheeks; her bow-shaped narrow eyes arched upwards. The more he scrutinized her features, the more he found them familiar. At length he burst out impatiently with the question, "Tell me, who are you? It seems to me that I have known or seen you somewhere."

"Two years ago in Kiev."

"Two years ago . . . in Kiev . . ." Andrei repeated, trying to call to mind every memory of his former life at the Academy. He gave her one more intent look and suddenly exclaimed aloud, "You are the Tatar woman—the servant of the lady, the Waywode's daughter!"

"Hush!" whispered the Tatar, clasping her hands imploringly, trembling all over, and turning her head round to see whether anyone had been roused by Andrei's loud cry.

"Tell me—tell me—where—why are you here?" said Andrei in a breathless whisper broken by inward emotion. "Where is your lady? Is she alive and well?"

"She is here in the town."

"In the town?" he almost shouted again, feeling all his blood rush at once to his heart. "Why is she in the town?"

"Because the old lord himself is in the town. He has been Waywode of Dubno for the last year and a half."

"And is she married? Speak! How strange you are! How fares she now?"

"She has not eaten for two days."

"How is that?"

"None of the townsfolk has had a crust of bread for a long time; all have long had nothing but earth to eat."

Andrei was dumbfounded.

"My lady saw you among the Zaporozhians from the town wall. She said to me, 'Go, tell the knight to come to me, if he remembers me; and if he does not, let him give you a piece of bread for my old mother, for I will not see my mother die before my eyes. Better that I should die first, and

50

she afterwards. Beseech him; cling to his knees. He, too, has an old mother; he must give us bread for her sake!' "

Many conflicting feelings kindled and burned in the young Cossack's breast.

"But how are you here? How did you come?"

"By the underground passage."

"Is there an underground passage?"

"There is."

"Where?"

"You will not betray me, knight?"

"I swear it by the Holy Cross!"

"Go, then, down that ravine and across the brook where the rushes grow."

"It leads straight into the town?"

"Straight into the town monastery."

"Let us go at once!"

"But first, in the name of Christ and the Holy Mary—a piece of bread!"

"Good; you shall have it. Stand here by the wagon, or, better still, lie down in it; nobody will see you—all are asleep. I'll be back directly."

And he went to the wagons where the provisions of his kuren were stored. His heart beat violently. All the past, all that had been pushed into the background by the rigors of his present Cossack life, now rushed at once to the surface and drowned the present. Again that proud woman rose before him, as from the dark depths of the sea. Once more there gleamed in his memory her beautiful arms, her eyes, her laughing lips, her thick dark nut-brown hair, falling in curls upon her breasts, and all her supple, maidenly body created in such perfect harmony. No, all this had never faded, had never died out in his heart; it had but given room for a time to other powerful emotions; but often, ah, how often had they disturbed the young Cossack's deep slumber! And often had he awakened and lain sleepless, without knowing why.

As he walked on his heart beat faster and faster and his knees trembled at the mere thought of seeing her again. When he reached the wagon, he had quite forgotten what he had come for; he raised his hand to his brow and rubbed it long, trying to recollect his errand. Then, he shuddered with fear from head to foot, struck with the thought that she was dying of hunger. He darted to one of the wagons and took several large loaves of brown bread under his arm; but immediately it occurred to him that such fare, though welcome to the plain taste of a robut Zaporozhian, would be too coarse and unfit for her tender constitution. Then he recalled that, the day before, the Koshevoi had cursed the cooks for using up all the buckwheat flour to make one supper, when there was enough for three meals. Sure of finding plenty of gruel left in the cauldrons, he took his father's gruel pot and went with it to the cook of his kuren, who was sleeping beside two tenpail cauldrons, with the coals still glowing under them. Peering into the cauldrons, he was astonished to find both of them empty. It must have taken superhuman effort to eat it all; the more so as their kuren numbered fewer men than the others. He looked into the cauldrons of the other kurens— nothing there, either. He could not but recall the proverb, "Zaporozhians are like babes; when there's little, they'll eat it; when there's much, they'll leave nothing."

What was to be done? There was, however, somewhere in a wagon of his father's regiment, a sack of wheaten bread, which was found when the bakery of the monastery was pillaged. He went straight up to his father's wagon, but the sack was not there: Ostap had put it under his head; he lay stretched out on the ground, making the whole field resound with his snoring. Andrei seized the sack with one hand and jerked it aside so sharply that Ostap's head dropped on the ground; he started up in his sleep, and sitting there with eyes closed, yelled at the top of his lungs, "Hold him, hold the Polish devil! And catch the horse! catch it!"

"Be quiet, or I'll kill you!" shouted Andrei in terror, swinging the sack at him. There was no need to do so, for Ostap broke off his speech, fell back, and gave such a snore that the grass around him trembled. Andrei looked cautiously about him to see whether Ostap's sleepy ravings had waked any of the Cossacks. One long-locked head rose in the nearest kuren; it rolled its eyes and soon dropped back on the ground. After waiting two or three minutes, he set out with his burden. The Tatar woman lay there hardly daring to breathe.

"Come, get up. Everyone is sleeping; do not be afraid. Could you carry one of these loaves if I cannot take them all?" With these words he slung the sack on to his back, pulled out another, full of millet, from a wagon on his way, even taking in his hands the loaves he had wanted the Tatar to carry, and, stooping somewhat under his load, he struck out boldly through the rows of sleeping Zaporozhians.

"Andrei!" called old Bulba, as they were passing him.

His heart stood still. He stopped and, shaking from head to foot, said faintly, "What is it?"

"There is a woman with you! Ay, I'll curry your hide for you when I get up! Women will lead you to no good!" So saying, he leaned his head upon his elbow and glared at the veiled form of the Tatar.

Andrei stood there, more dead than alive, not daring to look in his father's face. And when he did raise his eyes and look at him, he saw that old Bulba was asleep, his head resting in the palm of his hand. He crossed himself. His fear rushed from his heart still faster than it had assailed it. When he turned to look at the Tatar, she stood before him, heavily veiled, like a dark granite statue, and the glare of the distant conflagration lighted up only her eyes, glazed as the eyes of a corpse. He tugged at her sleeve, and both went on, looking back at every step, until at last they climbed down the slope of a deep hollow or ravine, along the bottom of which a brook snaked lazily, overgrown with sedge and studded with tufts of sod.

Once they reached the bottom of the ravine, they were well out of sight of the Zaporozhian camp. At least, as Andrei glanced back, he saw the bank loom behind him in a steep wall. On its crest waved a few stalks of steppe-grass, over which the moon rose like a tilted sickle of bright pure gold. The light breeze blowing from the steppe was a warning that little time remained till the dawn. But no distant crow of the cock was heard, for neither in the town nor in the devastated neighborhood had a cock been left for a long time past. They crossed the brook over a small log; the opposite bank appeared higher and rose more steeply. It seemed that this was a strong and naturally defended point of the town fortress, for the earthen ramparts here were lower, and no part of the garrison was seen behind it; yet farther on towered the thick wall of a monastery. The sheer bank was covered with a growth of rank weeds, and in the narrow strip of ravine between the bank and the brook grew reeds almost as tall as a man. On the summit of the bluff there could be seen the remains of a wattled fence, which had once enclosed a garden. In front if it grew some wide leaves, behind rose the rushes, the thistle, and the sunflower, which reared its head above the others. Here the Tatar shook off her slippers and went barefoot, carefully gathering up her skirts, for the spot was swampy and covered with water. Having made their way through the reeds, they stopped before a heap of brushwood and thistles. Pushing the brushwood aside, they revealed a sort of earthen arch—an opening not much wider than the mouth of a baker's oven. The Tatar, bending her head, went in first. Andrei followed, bending as low as he could, so as to pass with his sacks; and both soon found themselves in total darkness.

CHAPTER SIX

ANDREI SLOWLY groped his way through the dark and narrow earthen tunnel, following the Tatar and carrying his sacks of bread.

"Soon we shall see our way," said his guide, "we are coming to the place where I left my lamp."

True enough, a faint light gradually lighted up the dark earthy walls. They reached a small open space, evidently used as a chapel: at any rate, a narrow table, like an altar, stood near the wall, and above it was an almost entirely defaced image of the Catholic Madonna. A small silver icon-lamp hanging before it threw a faint light on the picture. The Tatar stopped and picked up the lamp she had left there on the ground; it was made of copper, with a tall, slender stem, and with snuffers, a pin for trimming the wick, and an extinguisher hanging from it on chains. She raised it and lighted it at the icon-lamp. The light grew brighter, and they went on, one after the other, now illumined by its blaze, now swallowed up by the coal-black murk, as in the paintings of Gerardo della Notte.

The knight's fresh and handsome face, glowing with health and youth, made a striking contrast with the pallid and emaciated face of his companion. The passage had become wider, so that Andrei could straighten himself. He looked with curiosity at the earthen walls, which reminded him of the catacombs of Kiev. Here, as in the Kiev catacombs, there were niches in the walls with coffins standing in some, while in others lay human bones, grown mouldy with the damp and crumbling into powder. Here, too, holy men had evidently sought refuge from the world, from its storms, sorrows, and temptations. In places it was very dark; sometimes there was water under their feet. Andrei was often obliged to halt to let his companion rest, as her fatigue made itself felt at almost every step. A morsel of bread she had swallowed had only caused pain in her stomach, and she frequently had to stand motionless for a few minutes before she was able to move.

At last a small iron door appeared before them. "Thank God! We are here," said the Tatar in a weak voice and lifted her hand to knock—but her strength failed her. Andrei, in her stead, gave a strong knock on the door. There was a hollow echo, which was a sign that beyond the door lay a wide-open space. The echo changed its tone as if thrown back by high vaults. In a minute or two, keys jingled, and someone seemed to be descending a flight of stairs. At length the door opened; they were met by a monk, who stood on a narrow stairway, with a bunch of keys and a candle in his hands. Despite himself, Andrei recoiled at the sight of a Catholic monk, who aroused such hatred and contempt among the Cossacks that they treated his brethren even more inhumanly than they did the Jews. The monk also started back when he saw a Zaporozhian Cossack, but a muffled whisper from the Tatar reassured him. He lighted them up the stairs, locked the door, and took them to the stairhead until they found themselves beneath the dark and lofty arches of the monastery church. Before one of the altars, with tall candlesticks and candles, a priest knelt, praying in a soft voice. On either side of him, also kneeling, were two young choristers, clad in purple mantles and white lace surplices, holding censers in their hands. He was praying for a divine miracle—that the town might be saved, that their fortitude might be strengthened, that patience might be sent them, that the tempter might be confused who inspired timidity in their souls and induced them to mutter against earthly misfortunes. A few women, ghostlike, were on their knees, supporting themselves by and even drooping their heads in utter ex-

haustion on the backs of the chairs and on the dark wooden
benches before them; a few men also knelt mournfully, lean-
ing against the columns and pilasters which upheld the side
arches. A stained-glass window over the altar was lighted
by the rosy hue of morning, and pale-blue, yellow, and crimson patches of light fell from it down on the floor, illumin-
ing the dim church. The whole altar, in its distant recess, suddenly stood out in a bright glow; the cloud of smoke from
the censers was tinted with all the colors of the rainbow.
From his dark corner Andrei gazed, not without surprise, at
the wonders wrought by the light. At that moment the majestic roar of the organ suddenly filled the whole church. It
grew deeper and more sonorous, rising and swelling into
heavy rolls of thunder; and then, all at once, it turned into
sublime music, and its singing notes soared high among the
arches, sweet as the voices of virginas; then once more it fell
into a deep roar and thunder, and was silent. But the thunder-
ous echoes long after cascaded vibrantly among the arches;
and Andrei, his mouth half open, marvelled at the majestic
music.

Just then he felt a tug at the skirt of his coat.

"It is time!" said the Tatar.

They went across the church, unnoticed by anyone, and
came out into the square outside. The blush of dawn had
long since touched the sky; all heralded the rising sun. The
square was empty; in the middle still remained some wooden
stalls, showing that, perhaps, only a week before a market
had been here. The street, unpaved as all others of its time
was simply a hump of dried mud. The square was surrounded by small one-stoned houses of stone or clay, their
walls displaying from top to bottom their latticed timber
frames. Such half-timber houses were common in the towns
of the day, and may even now be seen in certain parts of Lith-
uania and Poland. They were all covered with inordinately
high roofs, with a great many dormer-windows and air-holes.
On one side, almost next to the church, rose a taller building
quite distinct from the others—probably the town hall or a
governmental establishment. It was two stories high, and
above it, on two arches, towered a belvedere, where a senti-
nel was standing; a large clock-face was built into the roof.

The square seemed dead; but Andrei thought he heard a
faint moan. Looking about him, he saw at the opposite end
two or three people lying motionless on the ground. He

57

strained his eyes to see whether they were asleep or dead; and at that same moment he stumbled against something lying at his feet. It was the dead body of a woman—apparently a Jewess. She must have been still young, though her wasted and distorted features did not show it. On her head was a red silk kerchief; a double row of pearls or beads adorned her ears; two or three long locks fell in ringlets from beneath them on her shrivelled neck with its tightly strung veins. By her side lay a child, whose hand clutched convulsively at her lank breast and, finding no milk there, twisted it with its fingers in vain anger. It was no longer crying or screaming, and only the gentle heaving of its stomach showed that it had not yet drawn its last breath. They turned into a street and were suddenly stopped by a madman, who, seeing Andrei's priceless burden, sprang upon him like a tiger and clawed at him, shrieking, "Bread!" But his strength was unequal to his madness; Andrei pushed him back, and he crumpled up on the ground. Moved with compassion, Andrei threw him a loaf, which he seized and began to bite and tear like a mad dog; and soon, on that spot in the street, because he hadn't eaten for so long, he expired in horrible convulsions. Almost at every step they were startled by the ghastly toll of famine. It appeared that many, unable to endure their torments in their homes, had run out into the street, as if hoping by a miracle to find comfort in fresh air. At the gate of one house sat an old woman, and it was impossible to tell whether she was asleep, dead, or swooning; at least, she no longer heard or saw anything, and sat still, her head sunk on her breast. From the roof of another house, there hung on a rope a stiff, shrunken corpse. The poor wretch could not endure the sufferings of hunger to the last and had chosen to hasten his end by deliberately taking his own life.

At the sight of these startling proofs of famine, Andrei could not help asking the Tatar:

"Couldn't they really find anything to eat? When men are driven to extremity, well, there's nothing to be done but to eat what they had till then been squeamish about; they may feed upon creatures forbidden by the law—anything might then be used for food."

"All has been eaten," answered the Tatar, "all the animals. Not a horse, nor a dog, nor even a mouse is to be found in the whole town. We never stored any provisions in the town: everything was brought from the villages."

"But how, then, dying such a fearful death, can you still think of holding the town?"

"Ay, the Waywode might have given up, but yester-morning the colonel—the one in Budzhak—sent a hawk into the town with a note forbidding its surrender, and saying that he was coming to its rescue and was only waiting for another colonel that they might set out together. Now they are expected every minute. . . . Well, and here we are at the house at last."

Andrei had already noticed from a distance a house unlike the others, apparently built by an Italian architect; it was constructed of beautiful thin brick, and had two stories. The bay windows of the lower story were encompassed in lofty granite cornices; the upper story consisted of a series of small arches, forming an arcade; between them were lattices with coats of arms; the corners of the building were likewise adorned. A broad staircase, of painted bricks, came down into the square. At its foot sat two sentinels, who in a picturesque and symmetrical manner held with one hand their knees and with the other supported their drooping heads, looking more like statues than human beings. They neither slept nor dreamed, but, it seemed, were insensible to everything around them: they paid not the slightest attention to those who went upstairs. At the head of the stairs, they found a richly clad warrior, armed from head to foot, who was holding a prayer-book in his hand. He raised his weary eyes on them; but the Tatar spoke a word to him, and he dropped them again upon the open pages of his prayer-book. They entered the first chamber, quite a large one, which served either as a reception-room or an ante-room. It was filled with soldiers, lackeys, huntsmen, cup-bearers, and other retainers—indispensable to the dignity of any Polish magnate, whether of martial rank or of the landed gentry—sitting along the walls in various postures. There was the reek of a snuffed candle; two other candles in a pair of huge candelabra, nearly as tall as a man, standing in the middle of the room, were still burning, although morning had long since peeped in through the broad grated window.

Andrei stepped straight toward a wide oaken door, escutcheoned and lavishly carved; but the Tatar plucked at his sleeve and pointed to a small door in a side wall. Through this they gained a passage, and then a chamber, which he began to examine curiously. A streak of light which filtered through a chink in the shutters picked out a crimson curtain, a gilded cornice, and a painting on the wall. Here the Tatar gestured to Andrei to wait and opened the door into another room, from which flashed a ray of candlelight. He heard a whispering and a soft voice which made him quiver inside. Through the half-open door he caught a glimpse of a graceful female figure, with a long luxuriant braid of hair falling upon an upraised arm. The Tatar returned and bade him enter. He had no memory of how he entered and how the door was closed behind him.

Two candles were burning in the room; a lamp flickered before an image; beneath stood a tall table with steps to kneel upon while praying. But he had no eyes for these things. He turned away and saw a woman; she seemed to have been frozen or turned to stone in the midst of impulsive movement. It seemed as if her whole body had been suddenly checked in the act of springing towards him. And he, too, stood amazed before her. He had not thought to find her such as she was: she was not the same, not the girl he had formerly known; nothing about her was the same; she was twice as fair and enchanting now than she had been. Then, there had been something unfinished, incomplete about her; now, she was like a masterpiece after the final stroke of the artist's brush. She had been a giddy but charming girl; and now she was a woman in the flower of beauty. Her uplifted eyes shone with matured feeling—not hints of feeling, but feeling in all its fullness. The tears were not yet dry in them and filmed down with a lustrous moisture that struck straight to the soul. Her bosom, neck, and shoulders had reached the measure of full-developed beauty; her hair, which formerly had waved in light curls round her face, had now become a thick, luxuriant mass, part of which was braided and pinned to her head, while the rest fell over her bosom in loose and lovely curls, and reached down to her finger-tips. It seemed that her every feature had changed. In vain did he try to discover a single trait of those which had haunted his memory—not one did he recognize! Great as her pallor was, it did not mar her wondrous beauty, but rather added to it something impetuous, irresistible, and victorious. Andrei's heart was awed, and he stood spell-bound before her. She, too, seemed surprised at the appearance of the Cossack, who stood before her in all the beauty and power of youthful manhood; who even with his mighty limbs immovable betrayed an easy and careless freedom of movement; his firm glance shone with a clear sparkle; his velvety brows curved in a bold arch; his sunburnt cheeks glowed with the brightness of fiery youth; his young black moustache was as glossy as silk.

"No, I lack the power to thank you, generous knight," said she, her silvery voice shaking. "God alone can reward you; it is not for me, a weak woman—"

She cast down her eyes; her lids fell over them in snowy semicircles, fringed with long arrowlike lashes. Her lovely face bowed forward, and a delicate blush spread over it. Words failed Andrei. He longed to unburden his heart to her —to say all as ardently as it burned in his heart—but could not. He felt something stop his tongue, his words were soundless; he felt that it was not for him, bred at the Academy and in a war-like, migratory life, to respond to words like these—and he cursed his Cossack nature.

At that moment the Tatar slipped into the room. She had already cut into slices the bread brought by the knight, carrying it on a golden plate, which she set before her lady. The beautiful girl glanced at her, at the bread, and then raised her eyes to Andrei. In those eyes there was a world of feeling. Their eloquent look, telling of her sufferings and of her inability to express her emotions, Andrei understood better than any words. All at once his heart grew light; everything within him seemed to have been set free. The feelings and impulses of his soul, which till then a mysterious hand had held on a tight leash, as it were, were now released, at large, and eager to flow forth in an untamable torrent of words. But the beautiful girl turned of a sudden to the Tatar and asked anxiously, "And my mother? Have you taken some to her?"

"She is asleep."

"And to my father?"

"Yes. He said that he would come himself to thank the knight."

The girl took a slice of bread and raised it to her lips. With inexpressible delight Andrei watched her break it with her pearly fingers and eat it—and suddenly he recalled the man who, mad with hunger, had died before his eyes from swallowing a piece of bread. He paled, and seized her hand, crying, "Enough! eat no more! You have not eaten for so long that the bread is poison to you now!" And she let her hand fall directly and, like an obedient child, looked into his eyes.

61

If only words could express—but no; neither chisel, nor brush, nor the loftiest and mightiest speech has the power of expression what may be seen in the eyes of a woman, or the emotion of him who looks into such eyes.

"O my love!" cried Andrei, his heart and soul, and his whole being brimming over with emotion. "What need you? what will you? Command me! Set me the most impossible task in the world—I will do it even if I have to die to do it! Yes, that I will! And to die for you—I swear by the Holy Cross—will be so sweet—no, I cannot say how sweet! Three hamlets are mine, the half of my father's droves of horses, all that my mother brought my father, even what she conceals from him —all is mine! No Cossack has arms like mine; the hilt of my sabre alone would buy me the best farm and three thousand sheep. And all this will I renounce, throw away, burn, drown at one word from you, at a move of your fine black brow! I know that my speech, perhaps, is foolish, ill-timed, out of place; that it is not for me, after my life at the Academy and among the Zaporozhians, to speak in the manner of kings, princes, and the flower of noble knighthood. I can see that you are a creature of God unlike us all, and far below you are all the other wives and maiden daughters of gentility. We are not fit to be your slaves; only the angels in heaven are worthy of serving you."

With growing amazement, all ears, not letting fall a single word, the maiden listened to the impassioned speech, which, as a mirror, reflected a young and powerful spirit. Each simple word of this speech, spoken in a voice flying straight from the bottom of his heart, rang with power. She raised her lovely face towards him, threw back her troublesome tresses, and gazed long at him with parted lips. Then she was about to speak; but she checked herself suddenly as she recalled that the young man was a Zaporozhian, that his father, his brethren and country stood behind him, stern avengers; that terrible were the Zaporozhians besieging the town; that a cruel death awaited all within. And her eyes were suddenly full of tears; she seized a silk-embroidered kerchief and pressed it to her face, and in an instant it was all wet. Long did she sit there with her beautiful head thrown back and her snow-white teeth set on her beautiful underlip—as if she had suddenly felt the sting of a venomous reptile—with the kerchief on her face lest he should see her racking grief.

"Speak but one word to me!" said Andrei and took her soft

hand. A sparkling fire ran through his veins at the touch, and he pressed the hand lying without feeling in his.

But she kept silent, never taking the kerchief from her face and remaining motionless.

"But why are you so sad? Tell me, why are you so sad?"

She flung away her kerchief, brushed aside the long hair from her eyes, and broke into sorrowful speech, uttering the words in a low, quiet tone. Thus the breeze, rising on a beautiful evening, wanders through the thick growth of the water-rushes, and soft, melancholy sounds rustle, whisper, and tinkle forth; and the wayfarer, lingering in inexplicable sadness, strains his ears to hear them, and heeds not the dying evening, nor the gayly floating songs of the villagers returning home from their harvest labors in the fields, nor the distant rumble of the passing cart.

"Am I not worthy of everlasting pity? Is not the mother who bore me unhappy? Is not my lot a bitter one? Art thou not my merciless tormentor, O my cruel fate? Thou hast brought all to my feet: the highest nobles, the wealthiest lords, counts, and foreign barons, all the flower of our knighthood! All love me, and any one of them would have counted my love a great boon. I had but to wave my hand, and any one of them—the first in beauty and birth—would have been my mate. And with none of them didst thou bewitch it, not with any of the best warriors of our land, but with a stranger, with our foe. For what sin, O most holy Mother of God! for what sins, for what heavy crimes dost thou so relentlessly, so ruthlessly punish me? My days were passed in affluency and superfluity; the richest viands and sweet wines were mine. And what was it all for? To what end? That I might die a cruel death which even the meanest beggar in the kingdom is spared? It is not enough that I should be doomed to this horrible fate; not enough that before my end I should behold my father and mother, for whom I would willingly give my life twenty times over, die in intolerable torment. All this is not enough, but I must before my end hear words and see love such as I have never before dreamed of. My heart must be rent to pieces with his speech—my bitter lot must be made still bitterer—I must bewail my young life still more piteously—my death must seem even more terrible—and, dying, I must reproach thee, my cruel fate, and thee—forgive my sin!—most holy Mother of God!"

63

As she fell silent, a look of utter hopelessness and despair came upon her face; its every feature betokened gnawing grief, and all, from the sadly bowed brow and downcast eyes to the tears which quivered and dried on her softly glowing cheeks—all seemed to say, "There is no happiness in this soul!"

"Such a thing was never heard of!" cried Andrei. "It cannot be, it shall not be that the best and most beautiful of women suffer so bitter a fate, when she was born that all that is best in the world might bow before her as before a holy being. No, you shall not die! It is not for you to die! By my birth and by all that I love in the world I swear you shall not die! But if it should happen, if nothing—neither strength, nor prayer, nor courage—can turn away this cruel fate, then we will die together; and I will die first, I will die before you, at your lovely feet, and death alone will part us."

"Deceive not yourself and me, Sir Knight," she said, gently shaking her beautiful head. "I know, and to my great sorrow I know but too well that you may not love me; I know your duty and your faith. You father and comrades and country call you, whilst we are your enemies."

"And what are my father, comrades, and country to me!" said Andrei with a quick toss of his head, drawing himself up, as straight as a poplar on the river-bank. "If it comes to that —I wish to know nothing and no one! No one!" he repeated in the same voice and with that gesture which in the brawny, dauntless Cossack announces his determination to do an unheard-of deed impossible to another. "Who says the Ukraine is my country? Who gave it to me for my country? Our country is what our soul longs for, what is dearest of all. You—yes, you are my country! That country will I carry in my heart, will bear it there as long as I live; I defy any Cossack to tear it thence! And for that country will I barter, give up, and destroy all that is mine!"

Turned for a space to stone, like a beautiful statue, she gazed into his eyes, and then suddenly burst into tears and then, with that wonderful feminine impetuosity of which none is capable but an uncalculatingly generous woman born for the finest impulses of the heart, she flung herself on his neck, clasped him with her wondrous snowy arms, and sobbed aloud.

At that moment muffled cries, together with the sound of trumpets and kettle-drums, were heard in the street. But he heard them not. He only felt how her beauteous lips bathed him with the sweet warmth of their breath, how her tears streamed over his face, and how her fragrant hair, falling unbound from her head, wrapped him in its dark and glossy silk.

Just then the Tatar ran in with a cry of joy. "Saved! saved!" she cried, beside herself. "Our troops have come into the town; they have brought grain, millet, flour—and captive Zaporozhians."

But neither of the two heard whose troops had entered the town, what they had brought with them, or who were the captured Zaporozhians. Filled with feelings as are not enjoyed in this world, Andrei kissed the sweet lips that touched his cheek; and the lips were not unresponsive; they returned the caress. And in that mutual kiss each of them felt that which is given to a mortal but once in a lifetime.

And the Cossack was lost! lost to all Cossack knighthood! Never again will he see Zaporozhye—his father's hamlets— the church of his God! The Ukraine, too, will never again see the bravest of her children who undertook to defend her. Old Taras will tear from his scalp a tuft of his grey hair and curse the day and the hour when he begot a son to shame him.

CHAPTER SEVEN

NOISE AND commotion filled the Zaporozhian camp. At first, no one could understand how the troops had entered the town. Then it was discovered that the Pereyaslav kuren, encamped by the side gates of the town, had been dead drunk; it was therefore not at all surprising that half had been killed and the other half captured, before either realized what was afoot. While the neighboring kurens, awakened by the noise, were seizing their weapons, the troops had already passed through the gates, and their rear ranks beat back with their fire the sleepy and half-sober Zaporozhians who rushed after them in disorder. The Koshevoi ordered all to assemble; and when all stood in a ring and had fallen silent, their heads uncovered, he said:

"You see, gentlemen brothers, what has happened this night. You see what drunkenness has led to; you see how the enemy has shamed us. That's the kind of people you are: if your vodka allowance is doubled, you go on swilling till the foes of Christian warriors not only pull your breeches off you, but even sneeze in your faces without your knowing it!"

The Cossacks all stood with their heads hanging, conscious

of their guilt. Only Kukubenko, the ataman of the Nezamai kuren, made reply.

"Wait, Batko!" said he. "Although it's against the law to retort when the Koshevoi speaks before the whole army, yet the matter was not as you say, and therefore I shall speak. You've not been quite fair in blaming this Christian army. The Cossacks would have been guilty and deserving of death, had they got drunk on the march, in action, or during some hard, arduous task. But we've been sitting idle, loitering round the town. No fast, nor any other Christian exercise; how, then, could a man help getting drunk in idleness? There is no sin in that. Let us now show them that they can't fall upon innocent folk. We've beaten them well before, and now we'll beat them so that they won't get away with their lives."

The speech of the kuren ataman pleased the Cossacks. They raised their heads, which had been drooping lower and lower, and many nodded approvingly, exclaiming, "Kukubenko has spoken well!"

And Taras Bulba, who was standing not far from the Koshevoi, said, "How now, Koshevoi? Kukubenko seems to have spoken the truth, eh? What do you say to that?"

"What do I say? I say that it is a happy father that has begot such a son! It needs no great wisdom to utter words of reproach, but great wisdom it needs to utter such words as do not embitter a man in distress, but encourage and embolden him, as spurs embolden a horse refreshed by water. I was myself going to say a word of cheer to you, but Kukubenko has thought quicker of it."

"The Koshevoi has also spoken well!" rang through the ranks of the Zaporozhians. "Well said!" joined others. And the greyest of them nodded their heads, shook their silvery mustachios, and softly said, "Well spoken!"

"Now listen, gentlemen!" went on the Koshevoi. "To seize the fortress—may the devil take it!—by scaling or undermining it, as the Germans do, is not a fitting business for a Cossack. But judging by everything, the foe has entered the town without much provisions; he hadn't many wagons with him. The people in the town are hungry; they will gobble everything up at once; as for their horses—I don't know what they'll do about hay, unless some saint of theirs drops it down from heaven on to their pitch forks; God alone can tell, and their priests are only glib with their tongues. . . . For one thing or another, they are sure to come out of the town. So break up into three parties and cover the three roads before the three gates: five kurens before the main gate and three kurens before each of the others. The Dyadkiv and Korsun kurens will lie in ambush. Colonel Taras will also go into ambush with his regiment. The Titarevka and Timoshevka kurens will make up the reserve and stand on the right flank of the baggage-train, and the Shcherbinov and the Upper Steblikiv kurens on the left. And let those dare-devils who have the sharpest tongues go forward and incite the foe! The Poles are empty-headed by nature: they will not stand your jeers, and perhaps even today they will sally forth out of the gates. The *kuren atamans* must all look to their *kurens;* whoever hasn't his ranks full will fill them up with the remains of the Pereyaslav *kuren.* Look to everything. Give a loaf of bread and a cupful of vodka to one and all to clear their brains. But surely everyone must still be full up with yesterday's food, for, to tell the truth, you stuffed yourselves so that I wonder none of you burst during the night. And here is one more order: if any pot-house keeper sells a Cossack so much as a single cup of vodka, I'll have a pig's ear nailed to his forehead and hang him up by his feet. Now then, to work, brothers! to work!"

Thus ordered the Koshevoi; and all bowed to him from the waist and, their heads still uncovered, set out for their wagons and their camps; it was only when they had gone quite a long way that they put on their hats. All began to make ready: they tested their sabres and broadswords, poured powder from the sacks into their powder-horns, drew back and arranged the wagons, and selected the horses.

All the way to his regiment Taras wondered what had become of Andrei: had he been captured with the others and captured before he was awake? But no, Andrei was not the man to be taken prisoner alive. Still, he was not to be seen among the slain Cossacks. Taras was so lost in thought as he strode at the head of his regiment that it was a long time before he heard someone calling him by his name.

"Who wants me?" he said, recovering at last.

Before him stood Yankel, a merchant.

"Sir Colonel! Sir Colonel!" he cried in a hurried, broken voice, as though wishing to reveal a matter of no small importance. "I have been in the town, Sir Colonel!"

Taras stared at him, marvelling how he could have succeeded in getting in and out of the town.

"What devil took you there?"

"I'll tell you this minute," said Yankel. "As soon as I heard all that noise at daybreak, when the Cossacks began to fire, I snatched up my caftan and ran there at top speed without stopping to put it on. I slipped into the sleeves already on the way, because I wanted to find out as soon as I could what the noise was about and why the Cossacks had begun firing at daybreak. So I ran up to the very town gates, just as the last of the troops were entering the town. And there before his troop was Cornet Galendowicz. He's a gentleman I know: these three years past he has owed me a hundred chervontsi. I ran after him as though to claim a debt, and so got into the town with them."

"How so? You entered the town and wanted to claim a debt?" said Bulba. "And he didn't order you to be hanged like a dog on the spot?"

"By heavens, he did not want to hang me!" the merchant replied. "His retainers had already caught hold of me and thrown a noose around my neck, but I begged the gentleman to spare my life, and said I would wait for the debt as long as ever he liked, and promised to lend him more, if he'd help me to collect my debts from the other knights. For that Sir Cornet—I'll tell you all—has not a single chervontsi in his pocket; although he has hamlets and manors and four castles and steppe-land stretching well nigh up to Scklow, he has no more money than a Cossack—not a farthing! Even now, if the Breslaw Jews hadn't equipped him, he'd have nothing to go to war with. That was why he couldn't go to the Diet—"

"What, then, did you do in the town? Did you see any of our men?"

"I've not seen our Zaporozhians. I've only seen my lord Andrei."

"You've seen Andrei!" cried Taras. "Well, man, where did you see him? in a dungeon? in a pit? dishonored? bound?"

"Who would dare to bind my lord Andrei! He is such a grand knight now. By heavens, I hardly knew him! His shoulder-pieces all gold, his brassards all gold, his breastplate all gold, and his helmet all gold, and everywhere and everything gold. He shines, all gold, just as the sun shines in spring-time, when every bird is chirping and singing in the garden and the grass smells so sweet. And the Waywode gave him his

69

best saddle-horse; that horse alone is worth two hundred chervontsi!"

Bulba was petrified.

"But why has he put on this foreign suit of armor?"

"Because it's finer. And he rides about, and the others ride about; and he teaches them, and they teach him. Just like the richest Polish lord!"

"Who forced him to do this?"

"I do not say anyone has forced him. Does not my lord know that he went over to them of his own free will?"

"Who went over?"

"Why, my lord Andrei!"

"Went where?"

"Went over to their side; he is theirs all over now."

"You lie, you swine's ear!"

"How can I lie! Am I a fool that I should lie! Would I lie at the risk of my head! Don't I know that the man who lies to a lord will be hanged like a dog!"

"So it means from what you say that he has sold his country and his faith?"

"I do not say he has sold anything; I only say he's gone over to them."

"You lie, you accursed dog! Such a thing never happened on Christian earth! You lie, you cur!"

"May the grass grow on the threshold of my house if I lie! May every one spit on the graves of my father, my mother, my father-in-law, and father's father, and my mother's father if I lie! If my lord so wishes, I'll even say why he went over to them."

"Why?"

"The Waywode has a beautiful daughter—great God! what a beautiful daughter!"

Here the merchant tried as well as he could to make his face express beauty; he spread out his arms, screwed up an eye, and twisted his mouth, as if he had just tasted something delicious.

"Well, and what of that?"

"He did it all and went over for her sake. When a man's in love he is just like the sole of a shoe—soak it in water and bend it any way you like."

Bulba was lost in thought. He remembered that great is the power of weak woman; that many strong men has she ruined; that Andrei was by nature most vulnerable to her charms. And long did he stand motionless, as though rooted to the spot.

"Listen, my lord, I will tell all to my lord," said the merchant. "As soon as I heard all that noise and saw them going into the town gates, I caught up a string of pearls I thought I might use, for there are beauties and noble ladies in the town; and where there are beauties and noble ladies, I said to myself, they are sure to buy pearls, even though they have nothing to eat. So as soon as the cornet's men set me free, I ran to the Waywode's courtyard to sell my pearls, and I learned everything from a Tatar maid there. 'There'll be a wedding the minute they drive off the Zaporozhians; my lord Andrei has promised to drive the Zaporozhians away!'"

"And you did not kill the devil's son on the spot?" roared Bulba.

"Why should he be killed? He went over of his own free will. What wrong has he done? It is better for him there, so there he went."

"And you saw him face to face?"

"By heavens, I did! Such a glorious warrior! grander than any of them! He knew me at once, God bless him; and when I went up to him he at once said—"

"What did he say?"

"He said—no, first he beckoned to me, and only then said, 'Yankel!' and I said, 'My lord Andrei!' 'Yankel, tell my father, tell my brother, tell the Cossacks, all the Zaporozhians, tell everyone that my father is no longer my father, my brother no brother, my comrade no comrade, and that I will fight them all! Every one of them will I fight!"

"You lie, you infernal Judas!" shouted Taras in a rage. "You lie, dog! You crucified Christ himself, man accursed of God! I will kill you, Satan! Away with you, or stay and die here!" And with these words Taras whipped out his sabre.

The terrified man took to his heels instantly and ran as fast as his skinny, shrivelled legs could carry him. He ran a long time, without turning his head, through the Cossack camp and far into the open steppe, although Taras, seeing the folly of venting his wrath on the first comer, did not give chase at all.

He now recollected that on the night before he had seen Andrei walking through the camp with a woman; and he bowed his grey head, although he still would not believe that so shameful a thing could have happened, that his own son had sold his faith and his soul.

Finally he led his regiment into ambush and disappeared with it behind the only wood which had not yet been burned by the Cossacks. Meanwhile the Zaporozhians, foot and horse, advanced to the three roads leading to the three gates. One after the other the *kurens* marched: Uman, Popovich, Kanev, Steblikiv, Nezamai, Gurguz, Titarevka, Timoshevka; the Pereyaslav kuren alone was missing. Its Cossacks had drunk too deep of their vodka and had drowned in it their good good fortune. Some awoke bound in the enemy's hands; others never awoke at all but passed in their sleep into the cold earth; and Ataman Khlib himself, bereft of his trousers and upper garments, had found himself in the Polish camp.

The enemy's movements were heard in the town; all crowded on its walls, and a lively picture was presented to the Cossacks: the Polish knights, each one more handsome than the next, stood on the ramparts. Brass helmets adorned with swan-white plumes shone like so many suns. Others wore small, light caps, pink or sky-blue, with the tops tilted to one side, and coats with sleeves hanging behind the shoulders, embroidered with gold or ornamented with lace. Many had richly mounted sabres and muskets, for which those gentlemen must have paid a dear price, and a profusion of other finery was to be seen. In front of all, with a haughty air stood the Budzhak colonel in a red cap with gold braid. He was a heavy man, taller and stouter than all the others, and his costly and ample overcoat hardly contained him. On the other hand, by the side gates, stood another colonel—a small, dried-up man, with tiny piercing eyes that gleamed sharply from under their bushy brows. He turned about briskly to all sides, pointing energetically with his thin, dry hand as he gave his orders; it was evident that in spite of his diminutive stature he was thoroughly versed in the science of war. Not far from him stood a long, lanky cornet, with thick mustachios and a wealth of color in his face—a sure sign that he loved strong mead and gay revelry. There were many nobles to be seen behind him, who had all equipped themselves either with their own money, or from the king's treasury, or with money obtained from pawning everything they had in their ancestral castles. There were also a few spongers on the vain senators, whom these last took to dinner-parties for

72

greater show, and who filched silver cups from the table and the sideboard, and when the day's show was over, mounted the nobleman's coach-box. Yes, the people there were a mixed lot. Some had not the price of a drink on them, but all had dressed up for war.

The Cossack ranks stood quietly before the walls. There was not an ounce of gold about their dress, and it only shone here and there on the hilt of a sabre or the mountings of a musket. The Cossacks did not like a rich battle-dress; their coats of mail and garments were plain, and their red-crowned caps of black sheepskin dotted the field.

Two Cossacks rode out from the Zaporozhian ranks; one was quite young, the other older; both sharp of tongue, and no mean Cossacks in deeds either—Okhrim Nash and Mikita Golokopitenko. Behind them rode Demid Popovich, a thick-set Cossack, who had been for a long time at the Setch, had fought at Adrianople, and had gone through many an ordeal in his life: had nearly been burned at the stake, and had escaped to the Setch with tarred and charred head and singed mustachios. But Popovich had put on flesh again, curled his scalp-lock once more behind his ear, and grown thick mustachios as pitch. He, too, was a man of cutting words.

"Ha! Red coats on the whole army, but I swear they're white-livered inside!"

"I'll show you!" bellowed the stout colonel from above. "I'll put you all in chains! Give up your guns and your horses, you serfs! Did you see how I bound your comrades? Ho, there! Bring the Zaporozhians out on the wall for them to see!"

The Zaporozhians, bound with ropes, were brought to the wall. In front of them was Khlib, their *kuren ataman*, minus his trousers and upper garments, just as he had been taken prisoner in his drunken sleep. He bowed his head, ashamed of being seen naked by his own Cossacks and of having been captured like a dog in his sleep. His hair had almost turned grey overnight.

"Cheer up, Khlib! We'll rescue you!" cried the Cossacks from below.

"Cheer up, friend!" added Borodaty, a kuren ataman. "It's not your fault that they took you naked—misfortune might happen to any man—but they ought to be ashamed of exposing you to scorn without giving you a decent covering."

"You're a brave army when you have to fight with sleeping men!" cried Golokopitenko, looking up at the wall.

"Wait a bit, we'll cut off your scalp-locks for you," shouted those above.

"I'd like to see them do it!" said Popovich. Then, turning in the saddle, he glanced back at the Cossacks and added, "But why not? Perhaps the Poles speak the truth. If that potbelly up there leads them out, they will all have a good defense."

"Why do you suppose they'll have a good defense?" asked the Cossacks, knowing that Popovich was sure to have a joke ready.

"Why, the whole army might hide behind him, and you won't be able to get at any one of them with your spears because of his belly."

All the Cossacks laughed; and many nodded their heads for a long time and then said, "Good old Popovich! His words are enough to—" But the Cossacks had no time to finish.

"Away, away from the walls!" yelled the Koshevoi. For the Poles, evidently, could not stomach the cutting words, and the colonel had waved his hand.

Hardly had the Cossacks retreated, when grape-shot rained from the walls. All was in a bustle on the ramparts; the grey-haired Waywode himself appeared on horseback The gates opened and the troops sallied forth. In the vanguard rode hussars in well-matched ranks; then came a chain-mailed troop; then pikemen in armor; then a troop in brass helmets; then the highest nobles rode singly, each man dressed after his own taste. The haughty knights would not mix in the ranks with the others, and those of them who had no detachment to command rode apart with their own retainers. Then came more ranks, and after these rode the cornet; behind him were more ranks again, and the stout colonel on horseback; and in the rear of the whole army rode the little colonel.

"Don't let them range themselves!" yelled the Koshevoi. "Attack them—all kurens together! Leave the other gates! Titarevka kuren, attack the right flank! Dyadkiv kuren, attack the left! Kukubenko and Palivoda, fall on their rear! Break up their ranks! Scatter them!"

And the Cossacks charged from all sides, upset and confused their ranks, and broke in among them. They did not

74

even give the enemy time to fire; spears and sabres came at once into play. They were all bunched together and every man had a chance to show his mettle. Demid Popovich speared three plain men-at-arms and knocked two of the highest nobles from their horses, saying, "Good horses! I have long wanted to have such steeds!" And he drove the horses far afield, shouting to some Cossacks, standing there, to take care of them for him. This done, he again joined the melee, fell upon the dismounted nobles, killed one, and throwing his lasso around the neck of the other, tied it to his saddle and dragged him across the field, having relieved him of his sabre with a costly hilt and a purse full of money which hung at his girdle.

Kobita, a young Cossack and a good one, engaged one of the bravest Polish warriors, and they fought long together. They were grappling hand to hand. The Cossack got the better of his foe at last, threw him down, and stabbed him in the chest with his sharp Turkish dagger. But the Cossack did not escape either; just then a fiery bullet struck him on the temple. His killer was the highest of nobles and the handsomest of knights, the scion of an ancient princely house. Stately as a poplar, he darted here and there on his light bay steed, and many feats of princely valour did he perform; two Cossacks had he cut in two; he had brought down Fyodor Korzh, a good Cossack, together with his horse, shooting the horse and piercing the Cossack under it with his lance; many heads and hands did he chop off; and now he had shot the Cossack Kobita through the head.

"There's a man I'd like to try my strength with!" roared Kukubenko, the ataman of the Nezamai kuren. Spurring his horse, he rushed upon him from the rear, with such a loud and unearthly roar that all the men around shuddered. The Pole tried to wheel his horse round and face his foe, but his horse, startled by the terrible cry, bounded aside, and Kukubenko's musket ball hit its rider. It struck him in the shoulder-blade, and he fell from his horse. Even then he yielded not, and tried to strike back at his adversary, but his arm fell weakly beneath the weight of his sabre, and Kukubenko, taking his heavy broadsword in both hands, thrust it down his blanched mouth. The blade knocked out two of his sugar-white teeth, split the tongue in twain, shattered his neck, and went deep into the ground. Thus did he nail the knight for ever to the cold earth. His princely blood, red as a rose growing on a river-bank, spurted out in a fountain and stained his yellow, gold-embroidered coat. Kukubenko had already left him and cut his way, together with his men, into another part of the melee.

"Why, he has left such costly finery!" said Borodaty. The ataman of the Uman kuren, riding from his men to the spot where Kukubenko's victim lay dead. "I've killed seven nobles with my own hand, but such finery I have not beheld on anyone."

And Borodaty gave way to cupidity; he bent down to strip off the rich armor and had already seized a Turkish dagger set with jewels, untied a purse of gold from the belt, taken off the bosom a pouch containing fine linen, rich silver, and a cherished love-token—a maiden's curl; but he saw not the red-nosed cornet, whom he had already unhorsed and given a good deep slash to remember him by, fly upon him from behind. The cornet swung his sword with all his might and brought it down upon Borodaty's bent neck. The Cossack's cupidity led him to no good: his mighty head sprang away; the trunk fell headless, reddening the earth far and wide; and his stern Cossack soul flew to eternity, gloomy and indignant, and surprised at having so soon deserted so stout a body.

The cornet had hardly grasped the ataman's head by its scalp-lock, in order to fasten it to his saddle, when a stern avenger appeared.

As the hawk that soars in the sky and sweeps in wide circles on his mighty pinions suddenly hangs poised in the air, and then swoops down upon the wayside quail, so did Bulba's son Ostap swoop upon the cornet, flinging a noose about his neck. The cornet's red face grew purple as the cruel noose tightened round his throat; he seized his pistol, but his stiffening hand could not aim straight, and the bullet flew wide. Then Ostap unfastened the silken cord at the cornet's saddle, which he carried to bind his prisoners, and having bound the cornet hand and foot with his own cord, tied its end to his saddle and dragged him across the field, calling on all the Cossacks of the Uman kuren to come and render the last honors to their ataman.

As soon as the Uman Cossacks heard that their ataman was no longer among the living, they left the battlefield and ran to recover his body, and without delay began to deliberate as to whom they should select as their ataman. At length they said, "Why need we argue? We cannot find a better ataman than young Ostap Bulba. True, he's younger than any of us, but he has the judgment of an old man."

Ostap, doffing his cap, thanked all his Cossack comrades for the honor and did not refuse it, either on account of youth or of youthful judgment, knowing full well that it was not the season to do so in time of war; but at once led them straight into the battle and showed them all that they had not chosen him ataman for nothing.

The Poles felt that the battle was getting too hot for them, and retreated at a run across the field in order to form again at its farther end. The little colonel waved to the reserve of our fresh companies, stationed apart from the rest at the gates, and grape-shot flew thence into the Cossack crowds. But with little effect, for the shot only hit the Cossack oxen, which were gazing wild-eyed upon the battle. The oxen bellowed with fear and turned towards the Cossack camp, smashing the wagons and trampling many men underfoot. But Taras, rushing at this moment from his hiding place, threw himself with his yelling regiment across their way. The maddened herd, startled by the noise, turned round and swooped down on the Polish regiments, laying low the cavalry and crushing and scattering them all.

"Thank you, oxen!" shouted the Zaporozhians. "You served us on the march, and now you serve us in war!" And they attacked the foe with redoubled strength.

Many of the enemy were killed there. Many of the Cossacks distinguished themselves: Metelitsya, Shilo, both of the Pisarenkos, Vovtuzenko, and many more. Seeing that the odds were against them, the Poles hoisted a standard and shouted for the town gates to be opened. The iron-bound gates opened with a creaking sound and received the weary and dust-covered riders, flocking like sheep into the fold. Quite a few Zaporozhians made to follow them, but Ostap stopped his Uman kuren, crying, "Keep from the walls! From the walls, gentlemen brothers! 'Tis not well to go near them." And he spoke truly, for the enemy on the walls opened fire at them and poured down everything that came to hand and many of the attackers suffered. Then the Koshevoi rode up and praised Ostap, saying, "Here's a new ataman, yet he leads his kuren like an old one!" Old Bulba turned round to see who the new ataman was, and beheld Ostap sitting on his horse at the head of the Uman kuren, his cap tilted to one side and the ataman's mace in his hand. "There's a man for you!" cried Taras, gazing at him; and the old Cossack rejoiced and thanked the Uman Cossacks for the honor bestowed on his son.

The Cossacks were about to withdraw to their camp when the Poles again appeared on the town wall. But now their mantles were torn; many rich coats were spattered with blood, and dust covered the handsome brass helmets.

"Well, have you bound us?" cried the Zaporozhians to them from below.

"I'll show you!" the stout colonel shouted from above, repeating his former threat and shaking a rope.

And still the dust-covered, weary warriors continued to threaten each other, and the most hot-headed on both sides exchanged gibes.

At last all retired. Some, exhausted by the fighting, lay down to rest; others sprinkled their wounds with earth and ripped kerchiefs and costly garments stripped from the slain foe into bandages; others again, who were the least weary, gathered the dead and paid them the last tributes. Graves were dug with broadswords and pikes; the earth was carried away in caps and in the skirts of their coats; the fallen Cossacks were reverently laid in the ground and covered with fresh earth that the cruel ravens and eagles might not peck out their eyes. But the corpses of the Poles were rudely bound by the dozen to the tails of wild horses, which they turned out into the steppe, chasing them and whipping them on the sides. The maddened horses flew over hill and hollow, across ditch and brook, dragging the gory and dusty corpses of the Poles over the ground.

Then the kurens sat down in circles to their supper, and talked far into the night about their battles and the feats that it had fallen to every one to perform, and that would be sung till the end of time by posterity. Long they sat, and longer still sat Taras, pondering over Andrei's absence among the enemy's warriors. Had the Judas been ashamed to come forth against his own blood or had the merchant lied and Andrei been simply taken captive? But then he remembered that Andrei's heart was all too easily swayed by a woman's words; and he was torn with anguish, and vowed vengeance against the Pole who had bewitched his son. And he would have fulfilled his vow; he would not have looked at her beauty; he would have dragged her forth by her luxurious

78

hair across the whole field, in the sight of all the Cossacks. Her beautiful breasts and shoulders, white and gleaming as the never-thawing snows that cloak the crests of the mountains, would have beaten against the ground and become covered with blood and dust; he would have torn to pieces her supple, lovely body. But Bulba knew not what God had prepared for the morrow and, growing drowsy, he at last fell asleep.

The Cossacks still talked among themselves; and the sober and wakeful sentinels stood all night by the fires, keeping a vigilant look-out on all sides.

CHAPTER EIGHT

THE SUN had not risen when all the Zaporozhians were called to council. Word had come from the Setch that during the Cossacks' absence the Tatars had pillaged it, unearthed their treasures, killed or made prisoners all those who had stayed behind, and had set out with all the herds of cattle and droves of horses they had captured, straight for Perekop. One Cossack only, Maxim Golodukha, had escaped on the way from the Tatars' hands, stabbed the Mirza, unfastened the bag of sequins that hung at his sash, and on a Tatar horse and in Tatar clothes, for one day and a half and two whole nights, had fled from his pursuers; he had ridden his horse to death, mounted another, killed that one, too, and reached the Zaporozhian camp on a third, having learned on the road that the Zaporozhians were at Dubno. He could only manage to tell them of the misfortune; but how it happened—whether the remaining Zaporozhians had drunk too deeply after the Cossack fashion and had fallen drunk into captivity, and how the Tatars had discovered the spot where the army treasury lay hidden—he did not say. His strength spent, his whole body swollen, and his face burned and scorched by the wind, he fell on the spot and was instantly fast asleep.

In such cases it was a rule with the Cossacks to set out in pursuit of the abductors at once and endeavour to overtake them on the road, for the captives might soon be sent to the slave markets of Asia Minor, Smyrna, or the island of Crete, and God knows in what places the Cossack scalp-lock might not be seen. This was why the Zaporozhians had not assembled. All to the last man, they stood with their caps on, for they had not come to take orders from their atamans, but to deliberate as equals among themselves.

"First let the elders give counsel!" shouted some in the crowd.

"Counsel us, Koshevoi!" said others.

And the Koshevoi took off his cap, and speaking not as their chief but as their comrade, thanked the Cossacks for the honour and said:

"There are many among us who are older and wiser in counsel, but as you have honoured me, my counsel is this: waste no time, comrades, but go in pursuit of the Tatars, for you know yourselves what the Tatar is. He will not await our coming, but will squander his booty in a twinkling and leave no trace. So my counsel is—to set out. We have had good sport here. The Poles know now what Cossacks are; we have avenged our faith as best we could, and a starving town is of little use. And so my counsel is to go."

"Let us go!" shouted the Kurens in a mighty voice.

But such words did not please Taras Bulba at all; and still lower over his eyes did he draw his frowning, grizzly brows; like black bushes they were, growing on a high mountain peak and sprinkled with needly northern rime.

"No, your counsel is not good," said he, "you cannot say that. You have forgotten, it seems, that our captive comrades remain here in Polish hands. You seem to want us to leave our Cossack brethren to be flayed alive or quartered, and carted through the towns and villages, as was done with the chiefs and the best Russian knights in the Ukraine. Have they not desecrated all we hold sacred enough without that? What manner of men are we, I ask you? What manner of Cossack is he who leaves his comrade in misfortune, who leaves him to perish in foreign parts like a dog? If it has come to such a pass that no Cossack values his honour, and allows himself to be abused and his grey mustachios be spat upon, then let no one reproach me. I will stay here alone!"

All the Zaporozhians wavered.

"And could it be that you have forgotten, brave colonel," said the Koshevoi then, "that there are comrades of ours in the Tatars' hands, too, and that unless we rescue them now they will be sold into lifelong slavery to infidels, which is a fate worse than the cruelest death? Have you forgotten that they now hold all our treasures, won by Christian blood?"

The Cossacks pondered over this, not knowing what to say. None wished to bring infamy on his own head. Then forward stepped Kasyan Bovdyug, the oldest in all the Zaporozhian army. He was honoured by all the Cossacks; had twice been elected Koshevoi, and had been as good a Cossack as the best in the wars; but he had long grown old and had ceased to take part in campaigns; neither did the old warrior like to give advice to anyone, but loved to lie on his side in the Cossack circles and listen to tales of war and adventure. He never joined in their talk, but would listen to every word, and press the ashes with his finger in his short pipe, which never left his mouth; would sit long thus with his eyes half-closed, so that the Cossacks never knew whether he were asleep or still listening. He had stayed home during other campaigns, but this time the old Cossack could not help himself; he waved his hand in Cossack fashion and said, "Happen what will, I'll go with you; I may yet be of use to Cossackdom!"

All the Cossacks grew quiet as he now stepped forward before the assembly; it was a long time since they had heard him speak. Everyone wanted to know what Bovdyug had to say.

"The time has come, gentlemen brothers, for me to say my word!" he began. "Listen, children, to an old man. Wise were the Koshevoi's words; and as the head of the Cossack army, who is bound to protect it and preserve the treasures of the army, he could not have spoken wiser. That is so!

"Let that be my first word. And now listen to my second word. Here is my second word: Great also was the truth of what Colonel Taras said—God grant him a long life, and more such colonels to the Ukraine! The Cossack's first duty and first honour is to be true to the law of comradeship. In my long life I have never heard of a Cossack deserting or betraying a comrade. These Cossacks here and those taken at the Setch are our comrades; it matters not where there be few and where many: all are our comrades, all are dear to us. So this is my word: let those to whom the Tatar prisoners are dearer go after the Tatars, and let those to whom the Polish prisoners are dearer, and who do not want to desert a just cause, stay behind. Let the Koshevoi do his duty and lead one half after the Tatars, and let the other half choose a Lieutenant Koshevoi. And if you will but listen to a white head, no man is fitter to be the Lieutenant Koshevoi than Taras Bulba; none of us is his equal in valour!"

Thus spoke Bovdyug and was silent. And all the Cossacks rejoiced at this wise counsel from the old Cossack. All flung up their caps and shouted, "Thank you, Batko! You've kept silent for a long, long time, but you've spoken at last! Not in vain did you promise to be useful to Cossackdom—and so it has turned out!"

"Well, do you all agree to that?" asked the Koshevoi.

"Yes, we do!" shouted the Cossacks.

"Then the Rada is over?"

"Yes. The Rada is over," shouted the Cossacks.

Then listen, children, to my orders!" said the Koshevoi, stepping forward and putting on his cap, while all the Zaporozhians to a man took off their caps and stood uncovered, with eyes fixed on the ground, as was always their custom when an elder prepared to speak. "Now divide, gentlemen brothers! Whoever wishes to go, step to the right; whoever wishes to stay, to the left! Whither the greater part of his kuren steps, thither its ataman is to go; the lesser part is to join other kurens."

And they all began to cross either to the right or to the left. Whither the great part of a kuren went, thither its ataman followed, and the lesser part joined other kurens. It came out that the sides were almost equal. Those who wished to remain were nearly the whole of the Nezamai kuren, the entire Uman and Kanev kurens, and the larger half of the Popovich, Steblikiv and Timoshevka kurens. All the rest chose to go after the Tatars. Many were the brave and strong Cossacks on either side. Among those who volunteered to go in pursuit of the Tatars were Cherevaty, a good old Cossack, Pokotipolye, Lemish, and Khoma Prokopovich. Demid Popovich also went over to their side, for he was a restless Cossack and could never stay long anywhere; he had seen battle with the Poles, and now wanted to pit himself against the Tatars. There, too, were the kuren atamans Nostyugan, Pokrishka, Nevelichky; and many other brave and renowned Cossacks wished to test sabre and muscle in a battle with the Tatars. There were a good many worthy Cossacks among those who wished to stay behind: the kuren atamans Demitrovich, Kukubenko, Vertikhvist, Balaban, and Ostap Bulba, and many other stout and famous Cossacks: Vovtuzenko, Cherevichenko, Okhrim Guska, Mikola Gusty, Metelitsya, Ivan Zakrutiguba, Degtyarenko, Pisarenko, the second Pisarenko, and still another Pisarenko, and many, many other good Cossacks. All of them had travelled much: had roved along the Anatolian coasts, and across the Crimean salt-marshes and steppes, along all the rivers, large and small, that flow into the Dnieper, along its inlets and islands; had visited Moldavian, Wallachian, and Turkish lands; they had sailed all over the Black Sea in their double-ruddered Cossack boats; they had attacked, with a fleet of fifty boats, the richest and greatest ships, sunk a few Turkish galleys, and shot much, very much powder in their time. More than once had they torn up costly silk and velvet for foot-wraps. More than once had they filled the purses hanging at their belts with bright coins. And it would have been impossible to reckon how much property—enough to keep other men in comfort their whole lives—they had spent in drinking and feasting. They had squandered it all in true Cossack fashion, treating one and all and hiring musicians that all the world might be merry. Even now, few of them had no treasure— cups, silver goblets and bangles—hidden in the reeds on the Dnieper islands in order that the Tatar might not discover it, if by mischance he should fall suddenly upon the Setch; it would be difficult for the Tatar to find it, though, for the owners themselves had begun to forget where they had buried it. Such were the Cossacks who wished to remain and take vengeance on the Poles for their faithful comrades and the Christian faith!

The old Cossack Bovdyug likewise resolved to stay with them, saying:

"My years will not let me chase the Tatars; and here is a place where I may die a good Cossack death. I have long prayed God that when my time comes to die, I may die in battle for the holy Christian cause. And so it has come about. Nowhere could there be a more glorious death for an old Cossack."

When all had divided and lined up in kurens, in two rows, the Koshevoi walked between them and said, "Well, gentlemen brothers, is each side pleased with the other?"

"We are all pleased, Batko!" answered the Cossacks.

"Well, kiss one another and bid one another farewell, for God alone knows whether you shall ever meet again. Listen to your *ataman*, but do what is fit, what Cossack honor bids you."

And all the Cossacks, as many as there were, kissed one another. First the *atamans* began; patting down their grey mustachios, they kissed each other's cheeks and then they took each other's hands and held them in a long clasp. Each longed to ask the other, "Shall we ever meet again, gentlemen brother?" but they kept silent, and both grey-heads were lost in thought, while all around them the Cossacks were taking leave of one another, knowing that much hard work lay ahead for both sides. However, they decided not to separate at once, but to wait till it was dark, so not to let the Poles notice the decrease in the Cossack army. Then they all went to their kurens for dinner.

After dinner, those who had to take to the road lay down and fell into a long and deep sleep, as though foreseeing that this was their last sleep to be enjoyed in such blissful security. They slept till the sun set; and when the sun had gone down and it grew dark, they began to tar the wagons. When all was ready, they sent their wagons ahead and once more doffed their caps to their comrades before slowly following the wagons. The cavalry trotted lightly after the infantry, with never a shout or a whistle, and soon all vanished in the darkness. Not a sound was to be heard but the hollow thud of the horses' hoofs and the creaking of a wheel that was not yet going properly, or had not been tarred well enough in the dark.

The comrades they were leaving behind waved after them for a long time, although they could no longer see anything. And when they turned and went back to their places and saw by the light of the stars, which now glimmered brightly, that half the wagons were gone and that many, many comrades were no longer among them, their hearts grew sad, and all became thoughtful and drooped their heads.

Taras saw that the Cossack ranks had become mournful and that sorrow, unbecoming to brave men, had bent the Cossacks' heads, but he kept his peace, for he wanted them to get used to their sorrow at parting with their comrades, and made ready to rouse them all at once with a loud Cossack battle-cry, in order that good cheer might return to each soul and bring greater strength than before, of which the broad and powerful Slav nature is alone capable—for it is to others what the sea is to shallow rivers. When the weather is stormy, it roars and thunders and raises such mountainous waves as feeble streams can never raise; but when it is windless and quiet, it spreads its boundless glassy surface, clearer than any river, an everlasting delight to the eye.

Taras ordered his servants to unpack a wagon which stood apart. It was larger and sturdier than any in the Cossack baggage-train; its massive wheels were encased in double iron hoops; it was heavily loaded, covered with horse-cloths and strong ox-hides, and lashed with tarred ropes. It was laden with casks and barrels of good old wine, which had long lain in Bulba's cellars. He had brought it along in anticipation of a solemn occasion, in case a great moment should arrive when a battle awaited them worthy of being handed down to posterity, so that each Cossack, from first to last, might drink of the treasured wine in order that at a great moment great feelings might be inspired in every man. On hearing the colonel's command, his servants rushed to the wagon, cut the stout ropes with their broadswords, tore away the thick ox-hides and horse-cloths, and took down the casks and barrels.

"Take them all," said Bulba, "all there are. Take whatever you've got—a scoop or a bucket for watering the horses, a gauntlet or a cap; and if you have none of these, just cup your hands!"

And all the Cossacks, as many as there were, armed themselves with a scoop, or a bucket for watering their horses, or a gauntlet, or a cap, or, if they had none of these, just cupped their hands. And Bulba's servants, making their way among them, poured out the wine from the casks and barrels. But Taras ordered them not to drink until he should give the signal for all to drink together. He was evidently about to say something. Taras knew full well that however strong the good old wine might be and however capable of rousing a man's spirits, yet, if a well-chosen word were to go with it, the strength of both the wine and the spirit would be doubled.

"I regale you, gentlemen brothers," spoke Bulba, "not because you have made me your *ataman*, great though that honour is, and not because of our parting from our comrades; no, at another time to do both would be fitting; but this moment is not a fitting one. The battles before us demand much sweat and great Cossack valour! So let us drink, comrades, all together and before all else to the holy Orthodox faith, that the day may at last come when it shall spread over all the world, and that everywhere there might be but one holy faith, and that all infidels to a man may turn Christians! And let us then drink to the Setch, that it may stand long to the confusion of all infidels, that every year it may send forth gallant warriors, each better and handsomer than the other. And then let us drink all together to our own glory, that our grandsons and their sons may say that there were once men who did not betray comradeship and did not leave their friends in need. So to the faith, gentlemen brothers, to the faith!"

"To the faith!" boomed those standing in the nearest ranks.

"To the faith!" joined the back ranks; and all, both young and old, drank to the faith.

"To the Setch!" said Taras and raised his hand high above his head.

"To the Setch!" returned the front ranks in a deep-throated echo. "To the Setch!" said the old men softly, twitching their grey mustachios; and the young Cossacks, rousing themselves like young falcons, repeated after them, "To the Setch!"

And the steppe far away heard the Cossacks salute their Setch.

"A last draught now, comrades, to our glory and to all Christians living on earth!"

And all the Cossacks, to the last man in the field, drank the last draught to their glory and to all Christians that live upon the earth. And long the shout resounded among the kuren ranks, "To all Christians living on earth!"

Their cups were empty, but the Cossacks still stood with uplifted arms, and though their eyes gleamed merrily with the wine, they were thinking deeply. No longer of the gain and spoils of war were they thinking now, nor of those who would be lucky enough to take purses, rich arms, embroidered caftans, and Circassian horses. Like eagles perched on the craggy mountain-tops, from which may be seen the boundless sea, dotted, as with tiny birds, with galleys, ships, and every manner of vessel, bordered only by the scarcely visible coasts, with towns no bigger than midges, and woods as low as grass—like eagles they gazed out on the steppe, and on their fate darkling far and dim before them. The time shall come when all the plain, its wastes and its roads, will be strewn with their white bones, drenched with their blood and covered with shattered wagons, broken sabres and spears. Far and wide will their heads lie, with twisted and blood-clotted scalp-locks and drooping mustachios. The eagles, swooping down, will peck and claw out their eyes. But great will be the fame of that wide and bone-strewn camp of death! Not a single lion-hearted deed will be lost, and Cossack glory will not perish like a tiny grain of powder from a gun-barrel. The time shall come when the bandura-player, his grey beard falling upon his breast, a white-headed old man still full perhaps of ripe manly vigour, and with the spirit of a prophet, shall sing of them in deep, powerful words. And their glory will sweep the world, and all who are born thereafter will speak of them; for the word of power carries far, like the brass of a bell, into which the founder has poured much pure and precious silver, that its beautiful ringing might be borne afar through town and hamlet, palace and hovel, calling all men equally to prayer.

CHAPTER NINE

NO ONE in the town knew that half the Zaporozhians had set out in pursuit of the Tatars. From the tower of the town hall the sentinels had indeed noticed that part of the wagons had been driven into the woods; but it was thought that the Cossacks were preparing an ambush; the French engineer was of the same opinion. Meanwhile, the Koshevoi's words were borne out: the town was again faced with starvation. As was usual in past centuries, the troops had miscalculated their needs. They tried to make a sortie, but one half of the dare-devils who took part in it were instantly slaughtered by the Cossacks, and the other half driven empty-handed back into the town. The Poles, however, had taken advantage of the sortie and ferreted out everything: whither and why the Zaporozhians had set out; with what chieftains; which particular kurens; in what number; how many had stayed behind; and what their plans were—in short, within a few minutes everything was known in the town. The colonels took courage and prepared to give battle. Taras perceived as much from the noise and bustle in the town, and took prompt action, giving injunctions and instructions, forming the kurens in three encampments and surrounding them with wagons as with barricades—a stratagem which had often made the Zaporozhians invincible—ordered two kurens to go into hiding, and drove sharp stakes, broken guns, and stumps of spears into part of the field, where he intended to drive the enemy's cavalry if possible. When all was done to his satisfaction, he made a speech to the Cossacks, not to encourage and cheer them—he knew them to be spirited enough without that—but simply because he wished to unburden his own heart.

"I wish to tell you, gentlemen, what our comradeship is. You have heard from your fathers and grandfathers how highly esteemed our country has been by all: it caused itself to be known to the Greeks; took tribute from Constantinople; our towns were rich, and we had, too, our temples, and our princes—princes of Russian blood, not Catholic heretics. Of all this have we been robbed; all has perished. We alone remained, poor orphans, and our bereaved land, too, like the widow of a mighty husband. At such a time, comrades, we joined hands in brotherhood! This is what our comradeship stands upon! No ties are holier than those of comradeship! The father loves his child, the mother loves her child, and the child loves its father and mother, but that is something else: the wild beast also loves its young. But man alone knows kinship of the soul and not of blood. There have been brotherhoods in other lands, too, but none ever as on our Russian earth. A good number of you have spent many a year in foreign lands; you have seen men there, God's men like yourselves, and you have talked with them as with your own folk; but when it came to speaking from the heart, then you saw that they were wise men, but not like yourselves at all, that they were and yet were not men like yourselves! No, brothers, to love as the Russian soul loves—to love not with the mind, or anything else, but with all that God has given you, with all you have, and . . ." Here Taras waved his hand, and shook his grey head, and twitched his mustache, and then went on. "No; no one else can love like that! I know that strange ways have taken root in our land: there are those who think only of their wheat and hay, and their herds of horses; who care only for the safety of their sealed casks of mead in their cellars. They ape the devil knows what heathen customs; loathe their mother tongue, countryman speaks not with countryman; countryman sells countryman as brutes are sold in the market. The mean favor of a foreign king—not even of a king, but of a Polish magnate, who kicks them in the snout with his yellow boot—is dearer to them than any brotherhood. But even the vilest of these villains, no matter how low he has fallen for all his fawning and grovelling in the mud, even he, brothers, has a spark of Russian feeling. And it will flame up one day; and the wretch will wring his hands and tear his hair, loudly cursing his vile life, and ready to redeem his shame with suffering. Let them all know what comradeship means on our Russian earth! As for dying—why, not one of them could ever die as we are ready to die! Not one! Their mouse-hearted natures would never let them!"

Thus spoke the *ataman*: and when he fell silent, he still shook his head, grown silvery in Cossack deeds. All who stood there were deeply moved by his words; straight to their hearts did they go. The oldest in the ranks stood motionless, their grey heads bent; tears filled their aged eyes; slowly they brushed them away with their sleeves. Then all, as with one accord, waved their hands and shook their wise heads. Clearly, old Taras had stirred in them many of those dear and best-loved feelings that live in the heart of a man grown wise in suffering, toil, bravery, and the hardships of life; or in a pure young heart, which, though unacquainted with them, yearns for them with all the ardour of youth, to the eternal joy of their old fathers.

Meanwhile, the enemy was already coming out of the town; drums were rolling, trumpets were sounding; and the nobles, arms akimbo, were riding forth, surrounded by their innumerable retainers. The stout colonel gave his orders, and they bore down in a close mass on the Cossack encampments, arms raised threateningly, aiming their weapons, eyes flashing, their brass armor glittering.

As soon as the Cossacks saw that they had come within gun-shot, their long-barrelled rifles thundered in a volley, and they kept firing with never an interval. The loud thunderclaps resounded far over field and meadow, merging into a steady roar; the whole plain was shrouded in smoke; the Zaporozhians kept firing without pausing to draw breath —those behind loaded the guns for those in front, thus dumbfounding the enemy, who could not understand how the Cossacks fired without reloading. Already the smoke enveloping the two armies was so dense that nothing could be seen; none could see how first one and then another dropped in the ranks; but the Poles felt very well how thick the shot was and how hot the affair was growing; and when they fell back, to escape from the smoke and look around them, many of their men were found to be missing, though only two or three of the Cossacks were killed. And still the Cossacks went on firing off their guns without a moment's interval. Even the foreign engineer was amazed at their tactics, which he had never seen before, and said then and there, in the presence of all, "These Zaporozhians are brave fellows! That is the way battles should be fought in other lands too!" And he advised that the cannon should be at once turned on the encampments. The cast-iron cannon roared with their wide throats; the earth shook and hummed far about, and the smoke rose twice as heavy over the whole plain. The reek of powder was carried to the streets and squares of towns far and near. But the gunners had aimed too high, and the red-hot balls described too wide a curve. With a fearful screech, they rushed over the heads of the Cossacks and sank deep into the ground, tearing up and tossing the black earth high in the air. The French engineer was angry at such lack of skill, and undertook to lay the cannon himself, heeding not the Cossack bullets, which showered around him hot and thick.

Taras saw from afar that the whole Nezamai and Steblikiv kurens were in mortal danger, and shouted in a voice of thunder, "Away from the wagons at once, and mount your horses all!" But the Cossacks would not have had time to do both these things had not Ostap galloped into the midst of the foe; he knocked the weapons from the hands of six gunners but could not reach the other four, being driven back by the Poles. Meanwhile, the French engineer had seized a fuse in his own hand to fire off the largest cannon of all, such as none of the Cossacks had ever seen before. Its wide jaws gaped horribly; death lurked within. And as it fired, and the three others followed it, shaking the earth with their blast— much damage was done. More than one old mother will mourn her Cossack son, beating her withered bosom with bony hands, more than one widow will be left in Glukhov, Nemirov, Chernigov, and other towns. The poor woman will run every day to the market, grasping at every passer-by, staring into the eyes of each to see if the one dearest to her were not among them. But though many an army will pass the town, never will she find among them her dearest.

Half the Nezamai kuren was no more. As the hail suddenly lays low the field where every ear of grain shone like gold, so were they laid low.

How the Cossacks raged! How they all rushed forward! How did *Ataman* Kukubenko boil with ire when he beheld that the best half of his kuren was gone! In a twinkling, together with his remaining Cossacks, he cut his way to the very midst of the enemy's ranks. In his fury, he hacked to pieces as a head of cabbage the first man he met, unhorsed many a rider, piercing man and horse with his lance. He reached the gunners and captured one of the cannon. There he saw that the *ataman* of the Uman kuren and Stepan Guska were on the point of seizing the largest cannon. He left them there and wheeled with his Cossacks towards another mass of the foe. And wherever the Nezamai Cossacks passed, they left a street behind them; wherever they turned, they left a lane of slaughtered Poles. Their ranks could be seen getting thinner; they were mowed down in sheaves. Hard by the wagons fought Vovtuzenko, and in front Cherevichenko; by the more distant ones fought Degtyarenko, and behind him, the kuren *ataman* Vertikhvist. Two nobles had Degtyarenko already speared, and he was now attacked by an obstinate third. This antagonist was agile and stalwart, attired in rich armour, and accompanied by fifty retainers. Furiously he pressed back Degtyarenko, threw him to the ground, and swinging his sabre over him, shouted, "None of you Cossack dogs will dare to fight me!"

"Here's one that will!" said Mosii Shilo, springing forward. He was a brawny Cossack, had more than once been *ataman* at sea, and had endured many hardships of every kind. The Turks had once seized him and his Cossacks near Trebizond, and had made them all galley slaves, chaining them hand and foot and giving them no food for a week at a time, and nothing to drink but brine. The poor slaves endured all rather than renounce their Orthodox faith. But *Ataman* Mosii Shilo could endure it no longer; he trampled the holy law underfoot, wound the accursed turban round his sinful head, gained the Pasha's confidence, and became keeper of the keys and overlord of the slaves. The poor slaves were greatly aggrieved, for they knew well that when one of their own people forfeited their faith and joined their oppressors, his tyranny was greater and harder to bear than that of any infidel. And so it turned out. Mosii Shilo had them all bound by threes with new chains, lashed them down with cruel ropes which cut to the very bone, and slapped them unmercifully on the napes of their necks. But when the Turks, rejoicing at having obtained such a servant, began to feast and all got drunk, forgetful of their law, he took every one of the sixty-four keys and distributed them among the slaves, that they might unlock their chains, fling chains and fetters into the sea, take swords in their stead, and cut down the Turks. Rich booty did the Cossacks seize then; and they returned with glory to their motherland, and long did the bandura-players sing the praises of Mosii Shilo. He might have been elected Koshevoi, but he was a queer fellow. At one time he would perform a feat beyond the contrivance of the wisest; at another, folly took possession of him. He drank and feasted all his riches away, was in debt to everyone at the Setch, and on top of it all, stole like a common thief: one night he carried off a full Cossack's equipment from another kuren and pawned it to the pot-house keeper. For this shameful deed he was bound to a post in the market, and a bludgeon was laid beside him, so that every passer-by might deal him a blow according to his strength. But not a single Zaporozhian raised the bludgeon against him, for all remembered his past services. Such was the Cossack Mosii Shilo.

"Many here will beat you dogs!" cried he, attacking his challenger.

How they did fight! The shoulder-pieces and breast-plates of both bent under their blows. The devil of a Pole cut through Shilo's shirt of mail, reaching the flesh with his blade. The Cossack's shirt was dyed crimson. But Shilo heeded it not; he swung high his sinewy arm (an heroic arm it was!) and stunned him with a sudden blow. His brass helmet flew into pieces; the Pole tottered and fell, and Shilo went on cutting and hacking his stunned adversary. Tarry not to dispatch thine enemy, Cossack: "it is better to turn round!" The Cossack did not turn round, and one of his victim's men plunged a knife into his neck. Shilo turned round and all but reached his slayer before he vanished amid the smoke of gunpowder. The roar of guns sounded from every quarter. Shilo staggered, and realized that his wound was mortal. He fell on the ground, clasped his wound with his hand, and said to his comrades, "Farewell, gentlemen brothers, my comrades! May the holy Russian land live for ever, and for ever may it be honored!" And he closed his dimmed eyes and his Cossack soul fled from its body.

But there was Zadorozhny riding forth with his men, and Vertikhvist shattering the Polish ranks, and Balaban plunging into the fray.

"How now, brothers!" said Taras, calling to the *atamans*. "There is yet powder in the powder-horns? Cossack strength is yet not weakened? The Cossacks do not yield?"

"There is yet powder in the powder-horns, Batko! Cossack strength is yet not weakened! The Cossacks do not yield!"

And the Cossacks charged again and confused all the enemy ranks. The little colonel beat the assembly and ordered eight colored standards to be hoisted to rally his men, who were scattered over all the plain. All the Poles ran to the standards; but they had not yet succeeded in ranging themselves, when *Ataman* Kukubenko charged their centre again with his Nezamai Cossacks and engaged the stout colonel himself. The colonel could not stand his ground against him; he turned his horse about and fled at a gallop. Kukubenko chased him far across the plain, cutting him off from his regiment. When Stepan Guska noticed this from his kuren on the flank, he set out to intercept him, lasso in hand, head close to his horse's neck; choosing his moment, he threw the noose about his neck. The colonel's face grew purple; he clutched the rope with both hands, endeavouring to break it, but a mighty thrust drove a pike into his belly. And there, pinned to the earth, he remained. But neither did Guska fare any better. Before the Cossacks knew it, there was Stepan Guska held up on four spears. The poor devil had only time to say, "Let all our foemen perish, and may the Russian land rejoice for ever!"

The Cossacks glanced around, and there was Metelitsya on the flank, treating Pole after Pole to stunning blows on their helmets; on the other flank *Ataman* Nevelichky was charging with his men; beside the wagons Zakrutiguba was mauling the foe; and by the more distant wagons the third Pisarenko was repulsing a whole band. And farther on they had come to clutches and were grappling on the wagons.

"How now, brothers!" called *Ataman* Taras, galloping in front of them all. "There is yet powder in the powder-horns? Cossack strength is yet not weakened? The Cossacks do not yield?"

"There is yet powder in the powder-horns, Batko! Cossack strength is yet not weakened! The Cossacks do not yield!"

Bovdyug had already fallen from his wagon. A bullet had struck him just below the heart, but with his last breath the old Cossack said, "I sorrow not to part from the world. God grant every man such an end! May the Russian land be for ever glorious!" And Bovdyug's soul flew up to heaven to tell other old men long since departed how well they fight on Russian earth, and better still, how well they die there for the holy faith.

Soon after him, Balaban, the kuren *ataman*, dropped to the ground. Three mortal wounds—from spear, bullet, and heavy broadsword—had he received. He had been one of the most valiant Cossacks; in many sea expeditions had he been ataman; but the most glorious of all was his raid of the Anatolian coast. They had taken many sequins, costly Turkish goods, stuffs and clothing, but they came to grief on the homeward voyage, falling in, poor devils, with Turkish cannon. A broadside from the Turk sent half their boats spinning and capsized them, drowning more than one Cossack, though the rushes tied to their sides saved the boats from sinking. Balaban rowed off as fast as his oars could carry him, stopping in the face of the sun, so that the Turk could not see him. All night long they baled out the water with their buckets and caps and patched up the shot-holes; they cut up their wide Cossack trousers for sails and, sailing off at full speed, outran the swiftest Turkish ship. Not only did they arrive without mishap, but brought a gold-embroidered chasuble for the Archimandrite of the Mezhigorsk Monastery in Kiev and a setting of pure silver for the Church of the Intercession of the Holy Virgin, at Zaporozhye. Long did the bandura-players sing of Cossack luck. Now, in the agony of death, he bent his head and said quietly, "I think, gentlemen brothers, I am dying a noble death: I have cut down seven, piked nine. I have ridden over many, and how many I shot I cannot remember. May our Russian land flourish for ever!" And his soul flew away.

Cossacks, Cossacks! Abandon not the flower of your chivalry! Already is Kukubenko surrounded; already but seven men are left of the Nezamai kuren; and they, too, are already at the limit of their strength, and Kukubenko's garments are already stained with blood.

Taras himself, seeing his plight, hastened to his rescue. But the Cossacks arrived too late; a spear pierced Kukubenko just below the heart before the foe around him could be driven off. He sank into the arms of the Cossacks who held him up, and his young blood gushed forth in a stream, like priceless wine brought from the cellar in a glass vessel by careless servants, who, stumbling on the threshold, break the precious flask; the wine flows out over the ground to the last drop, and the master comes running and tearing his hair, for he had preserved it for the happiest moment of his life, hoping that God would grant him, in his old age, a meeting with a friend of his youth, that they might drink together to bygone times when a man made merry in another and a better way. Now Kukubenko rolled his eyes around and said, "I thank God, my comrades, that I die before your eyes. May those who live after us be better men than we, and may our Russian land, beloved of Christ, be ever beautiful!"

And away flew his young soul. The angels took it in their arms and bore it to heaven. He will have a good time there. "Sit ye down at my right hand, Kukubenko!" will Christ say to him. "Thou hast not betrayed the comrades, nor done any dishonourable deed, nor forsaken a man in distress; thou hast protected and preserved my Church!"

Kukubenko's death saddened them all. The Cossack ranks were growing thinner; many, many brave men were missing; yet still they kept their ground and stood firm.

"How now, brothers!" called Taras to the remaining kurens. "There is yet powder in the powder-horns? Your sabres are not yet blunt? Cossack strength is not yet wearied? The Cossacks do not give way?"

"There is still powder enough, Batko! Our sabres are still sharp! Cossack strength is yet not wearied! The Cossacks do not give way!"

And once more they charged forward, as though they had suffered no loss. Already only three kuren *atamans* remained alive. Crimson streams of blood flowed everywhere; the bodies of the Cossacks and their foemen, heaped together, were like tall bridges above them. Taras glanced up at the sky, and lo! already a string of falcons stretched across the heavens. What a feast they would have! And there Metelitsya was being raised on a spear. And there rolled the head of the second Pisarenko, with fluttering eyelids. And there Okhrim Guska doubled up and crashed to the ground, hewn in four pieces.

"Now!" said Taras and waved his kerchief. Ostap caught the signal and came hurtling from his hidingplace, dealing a mighty blow to the enemy's flank. The Poles gave way before this onslaught, and he drove them on and on, straight towards that part of the field which was studded with stakes and stumps of spears. The horses stumbled and fell, and their riders flew over their heads. At that moment the Korsun Cossacks, who stood farthest behind the wagons, seeing that the foe was within gun-shot, thundered away all of a sudden with their guns. The Poles were thrown into confusion, they lost their heads completely; and the Cossacks took heart. "The victory is ours!" shouted the Zaporozhians on all sides; they blew their trumpets and unfurled the banner of victory. The vanquished Poles were running and hiding everywhere.

"No, the victory is not yet ours!" said Taras, looking towards the town gates; and truly did he speak. The gates opened, and out dashed a regiment of hussars, the pick of the cavalry. Every rider was mounted on a matched chestnut charger, large in size but swift of foot. Ahead galloped a knight, the bravest and handsomest of all. His black lock waved from beneath his brass helmet; a rich scarf fluttered from his arm, embroidered by the hand of the fairest beauty. Taras was struck dumbfounded when he saw that it was Andrei. He was entirely lost in the heat and fire of battle, eager to prove himself deserving of the token tied round his arm; he flew like a young greyhound, the handsomest, swiftest, and youngest of the pack; urged by the tally-ho of the skilled huntsman, he darts forward, legs outstrung in a straight line and body slantwise, tearing up the snow and a score of times outrunning the hare in the heat of the chase. Old Taras stopped and watched how he cleared his way, scattering those in front, hewing them down, and striking to right and left. Unable to stand the sight, Taras roared, "What! Your own comrades? You would kill your own comrades, you devil's son?"

But Andrei saw not who were before him, friends or enemies. Nothing did he see, but—curls, long curls, and a bosom white as the river swan's, and a snowy neck, and shoulders, and all that was created for mad, passionate kisses.

"Hey there, children! Do you but lure him to yonder wood for me!" yelled Taras. In a flash, thirty of the swiftest Cossacks rode forth to fulfill his command. They settled their tall caps more firmly on their heads and raced to meet the hussars. They attacked the foremost in flank, confused them, cut them off from the ranks behind, and meted out a few hearty blows, while Golokopitenko brought down the flat of his sword on Andrei's back; and then all fled from the hussars at the top of their Cossack speed. How heated did Andrei become! How his young blood did boil in every vein! Digging his sharp spurs into his horse's flanks, he set off at his utmost speed after the Cossacks, with never a backward glance, not knowing that only twenty of his men were able to keep up with him. The Cossacks rode at full gallop and turned straight towards the wood. Andrei hurtled forward on his steed and had almost overtaken Golokopitenko, when a strong hand seized his bridle. Andrei whirled round: before him was Taras! He trembled all over and turned suddenly pale. . . .

Thus does a schoolboy—who, having offended a classmate and receiving a blow with a ruler, flares up, springs up in a fury from his bench to chase his terrified classmate, wishing to tear him to pieces, and then runs into the teacher entering the classroom—suddenly quell his frantic impulse and subdue his impotent wrath. And so, in one instant did Andrei's wrath vanish, as though it had never been. And all he saw before him was his terrible father.

"Well, what are we to do now?" said Taras, gazing straight into his eyes.

But Andrei knew not what to say, and remained silent, with his eyes fixed on the ground.

"Well, son, have the Poles helped you?"

Andrei made no answer.

"So, to betray—to betray your faith? to betray your comrades? Well, then! Get down from your horse!"

Obedient as a child, he dismounted and stood before Taras more dead than alive.

"Stand still, do not move! I begot you—and I will kill you!" said Taras, and stepping back, he took his gun from his shoulder.

White as a sheet stood Andrei; his lips moved gently as he uttered a name; it was not the name of his country, nor of his mother, nor of his brethren, but the name of the beautiful Pole. Taras fired.

As the ear of wheat cut down by the sickle, as the young lamb that feels the lethal steel at its heart, he dropped his head and fell on the grass without a word.

The murderer of his son stood still and gazed long upon the lifeless body. He was handsome even in death: his manly face, so short a time ago filled with power and with irresistible fascination for every woman, was still marvellously beautiful; his black brows, like sombre crepe, set off the pallor of his features.

"What a Cossack he might have been!" said Taras. "Tall of stature, black-browed, the face of a gentleman, and an arm strong in battle. And he has perished, perished ignominiously, like a vile dog!"

"Batko, what have you done? Was it you who killed him?" said Ostap, riding up at this moment.

Taras nodded his head.

Ostap gazed intently into the dead eyes. He was filled with sorrow for his brother, and said at once, "Let us bury him decently, Batko, that no enemy may do any dishonour to him, nor the birds of prey tear his body."

"They'll bury him without our help!" said Taras. "He'll have plenty of weepers and mourners!"

For a minute or two he reflected whether he should leave him a prey to the wolves or show respect for his knightly valour, which the brave are bound to honour in every man. Then he saw Golokopitenko galloping towards him.

"Woe to us, *Ataman!* The Poles have grown stronger; fresh reinforcements have come to their rescue!"

Hardly had Golokopitenko done speaking, when Vovtuzenko galloped up.

"Woe to us, *Ataman!* A fresh force is coming up!"

Hardly had Vovtuzenko done speaking, when Pisarenko ran up on foot.

"Where are you, Batko? The Cossacks are seeking you. Already *Ataman* Nevilichky is killed, and Zadorozhny, and Cherevichenko! But the Cossacks stand firm, and will not die till they have seen you. They want you to see them at the hour of death."

"To horse, Ostap!" cried Taras, and hastened to his Cossacks, to look once more upon them and to let them behold their *ataman* before death's hour.

But before they could ride out of the wood, the enemy surrounded it on all sides, and horsemen armed with spears and sabres appeared everywhere between the trees.

"Ostap! Ostap! Don't give in!" shouted Taras, and unsheathing his sabre, he struck out on all sides.

Six men suddenly sprang upon Ostap; but they had chosen an evil hour: the head of one flew off; another went heels over head as he fell back; a spear pierced the ribs of the third; a fourth, more daring, dodged a bullet, and the fiery ball hit his horse's chest; the maddened steed reared and fell on the ground, crushing his rider under him.

"Well done, son! Well done, Ostap!" shouted Taras. "I'll deal with them in a like manner!"

And he kept beating off his assailants. Right and left he struck, showering his favours on the heads about him, never leaving his eyes off Ostap ahead. Then he saw no less than eight men closing round Ostap.

"Ostap! Ostap! Don't give in!"

But they had already overpowered Ostap. Now a lasso was thrown about his neck—now they were trussing him up—now they were bearing him away.

"Ostap! Oh, Ostap!" shouted Taras, fighting his way towards him and hacking everyone who crossed his path into mincemeat. "Ostap! Oh, Ostap!"

But then he himself was struck by something, like a heavy stone. Everything whirled and turned round before his eyes. For a moment there flashed before him a confusion of heads, spears, smoke, sparks of fire, and then—a fleeting vision of leafy boughs. And down he crashed like a felled oak, and a heavy mist covered his eyes.

CHAPTER TEN

"HOW LONG I've slept!" said Taras, coming to his senses as after a heavy drunken sleep and trying to make out the objects about him. A fearful weakness locked his limbs. The walls and corners of a strange room danced dimly before him. At last he saw that Tovkach was seated before him, apparently listening to his every breath.

"Yea," thought Tovkach, "you might well have slept for ever!" But he said nothing, only shook his finger, commanding silence.

"But tell me, where am I now?" asked Taras, gathering his thoughts and endeavouring to recall what had happened.

"Keep your peace!" cried his comrade sternly. "What more do you want to know? Don't you see that you are all cut up? 'Tis a fortnight now we've been galloping with you, without stopping to take breath, and you've been in a fever and babbling nought but rubbish. 'Tis the first time you've slept quietly. So keep your peace if you don't wish to bring woe upon your head."

But Taras still tried to collect his thoughts and to recall what had happened.

"Why, I was surrounded and nearly captured by the Poles! I had no way of fighting through that crowd!"

"Hold your tongue, I tell you, you devil's son!" shouted Tovkach crossly, as a nurse driven beyond patience cries out to a restless, naughty child. "What good will it do you to know how you escaped? It is enough that you did escape. There were men who would not desert you—that's all you need know! We have still many nights of hard riding before us. Do you think you are priced as a common Cossack? No, they have set a price of two thousand gold pieces on your head."

"And what of Ostap?" cried Taras suddenly; he strove to rise, and all at once remembered how Ostap had been seized and bound before his eyes, and that he must now be in Polish hands.

His old head was filled with grief. He tore the bandages from all his wounds, flung them far from him, tried to say something—and began to rave instead; fever and delirium again came over him, and he broke into a stream of incoherent, senseless words. His faithful comrade stood over him, swearing and showering gruff reproaches upon him. Then he took hold of his legs and arms, swaddled him up like a child, replaced all his bandages, wrapped him in an ox-hide, bound him up, and, roping him to his saddle, galloped away with him.

"I'll get you there dead or alive! I'll not let the Poles mock your Cossack bone and blood, tear your body to pieces, and cast them into the river. And if an eagle is to peck your eyes out of your skull, let it be an eagle of the steppe, our eagle, and not a Polish one, not one that flies from Polish soil. Dead or alive I'll get you to the Ukraine!"

Thus spoke the faithful comrade. Day and night he galloped without rest, and brought him, still unconscious, to the Zaporozhian Setch. There he untiringly doctored him with herbs and lotions; he sought out a skilful Jewess, who for a whole month made him drink various potions; and at last Taras began to mend. Either the medicines or his iron constitution gained the upper hand, and in a month and a half he was on his feet again, his wounds healed, and only the sabre scars showing how dangerously wounded he had been. But he had grown noticeably gloomy and sorrowful. Three deep furrows cut across his brow, never to leave it. He looked about him now: all was new in the Setch; all his old comrades were dead. Not one remained of those who had stood up for the just cause, for the faith and for brotherhood.

And those who had gone with the Koshevoi in pursuit of the Tatars—they, too, had long since disappeared: all had laid down their heads, all had perished—some in battle, others in the hungry, waterless salt-marshes of the Crimea, others in shameful captivity; and the former Koshevoi and all the old comrades were no more; and weeds were growing over what was once seething Cossack strength. It seemed to him that there had been a great, riotous feast; all the dishes had been smashed in pieces; not a drop of wine was left anywhere; the guests and servants had pillaged all the costly cups and goblets; and now he stood in dejection, thinking, "I would there had been no feast at all." In vain did they try to divert and cheer Taras; in vain did the long-bearded, grey bandura-players come by twos and threes to glorify his Cossack deeds. Grim and cold, he stared blankly at everything; and on his stolid face an unquenchable sorrow appeared at times, and, quietly drooping his head, he would moan, "My son! My Ostap!"

The Zaporozhians set out on a raid by sea. Two hundred boats were launched on the Dnieper; and Asia Minor saw them, with their shaven heads and long scalp-locks, as they put its thriving shores to fire and sword; saw the turbans of its people strewn, like its countless flowers, over the blood-drenched fields, and floating along its coast. It saw many broad Zaporozhian trousers, besmeared with tar, and many brawny hands with black Cossack whips. The Zaporozhians devoured all the grapes and destroyed all the vineyards, left dung-hills in the mosques, used rich Persian shawls for sashes to gird their grimy coats. Long afterwards were their short Zaporozhian pipes to be found in those parts. Merrily they sailed back. A ten-gun Turk overtook them and with one broadside scattered their frail boats like birds. One-third of them were drowned in the depths of the sea; but the rest joined together again and reached the mouth of the Dnieper with twelve kegs full of sequins. But all this no longer interested Taras. He would go to the meadows and steppes as if to hunt, but his charge remained unfired. Laying down his musket, he would seat himself by the seashore, full of anguish. Long he sat there with drooping head, ever repeating, "My Ostap! My Ostap!" Before him the Black Sea spread and sparkled; the seagull shrieked in the distant reeds; his white mustachios gleamed like silver, and the tears dropped one after another.

At last Taras could bear it no longer. "Come what will, but I'll go and find out what has befallen him. Is he alive? or in his grave? or dead and unburied? I'll know, cost what it may!"

Within a week he was already in Uman, armed and mounted, with lance, sabre, travelling-flask at his saddle, a pot of gruel, cartridges, horse-shackles, and other equipment. He rode straight towards an ill-kept filthy hut, the tiny windows of which were almost invisible, so black were they with soot; its chimney was stopped with rags, and its roof was full of holes and covered with sparrows. A heap of rubbish lay before the very door. From one of the windows peered the head of a Jewess in a head-dress trimmed with discoloured pearls.

"Husband at home?" asked Bulba, getting down from his horse and fastening the bridle to an iron hook by the door.

"At home," said the Jewess, and hastened out at once with a scoop of wheat for the horse and a flagon of beer for the knight.

"Well, where is he?"

"He is in the other room, praying," answered the Jewess, curtseying and wishing Bulba good health as he raised the flagon to his lips.

"Stay here, and feed and water my horse, while I go and speak with him alone. I have business with him."

The man was none other than Yankel. He had already settled there as lease-holder and pot-house keeper.

Taras stepped into the room. The merchant was praying, his head covered with a shroud, and he had just turned to spit for the last time, according to his religion, when his eyes suddenly lighted on Bulba, who had stopped behind him. The two thousand offered for Bulba's head flashed before his eyes; but he was ashamed of his cupidity and strove to quell within him the eternal thought of gold.

"Hello, Yankel!" said Taras to the man, who began bowing to him and warily locked the door in order that nobody should see them together. "I saved your life; the Zaporozhians would have torn you to pieces like a dog; now it is your turn—now you must do me a service."

"What service? If it is a service I can do you, why shouldn't I?"

"Don't waste time on words. Take me to Warsaw."

"To Warsaw? How so, to Warsaw?" said Yankel. His brows and shoulders rose in amazement.

"Don't waste time on words. Take me to Warsaw. Come what will, I want to see him once more, and speak but one word to him."

"One word to whom?"

"To him, to Ostap, to my son!"

"Does not my lord know that already—"

"I know all. They've offered two thousand ducats for my head. They know its value, the fools! I'll give you five thousand. Here are two thousand now"—Bulba poured out two thousand ducats from a leather purse—"and the rest when I return."

"Oh, what beautiful coins! Oh, good coins!" he said turning a ducat in his fingers and testing it with his teeth. "Methinks the man whom my lord relieved of these fine ducats did not live an hour longer, but went straight to the river and drowned himself, after losing these beautiful ducats."

"I'd have not asked you; I might, perhaps, have gone to Warsaw alone, but the accursed Poles might recognize and seize me, for I am no good at plotting, and you are made for it. You could cheat the Devil himself; you know every trick —that is why I've come to you! And, besides, in Warsaw, I could do nothing alone. Now go and get your wagon ready, and take me there!"

"And does my lord think that I can go and harness my mare, and cry 'gee up, Grey'? Does my lord think that I can take him just as he is, without hiding him?"

"Well, hide me, hide me as you like! In an empty barrel, perhaps, eh?"

"Oh, oh! And does my lord think that he can be hidden in a barrel? Does my lord not know that everyone will think that there is vodka in the barrel?"

"Well, let them think it's vodka."

"What! Let them think it is vodka?" said the merchant, and clutched his ears with both hands, and then raised them both on high.

"Well, what frightens you now?"

"Why, does my lord not know that God made vodka so that every man might drink it? All the men there are fond of dainties, they all have a sweet tooth; every squire will run for hours after the barrel, bore a hole in it, and will at once see that nothing flows out, and say, 'A merchant would not carry an empty barrel; there must be something amiss here! Seize him, bind him, take all his money, away to prison with him!' For all that is ever wrong is blamed on the Jews, for the Jew is taken for a dog by all; for they think he's not even a man if he's Jewish."

"Well, put me in a wagon with fish."

"I cannot, my lord; by heaven, I cannot. In all Poland the people are as hungry as hounds; they'll steal all the fish and discover my lord."

"Well, put me on the devil's back then, but take me there!"

"Hear me! Hear me, my lord!" said Yankel, pulling up his sleeves, and coming up to him with arms outstretched. "Here is what we will do. Fortresses and castles are now being built everywhere. French engineers have come from abroad, and so a great deal of brick and stone is being carried over the roads. Let my lord lie on the bottom of the wagon, and I'll lay bricks over him. My lord looks hale and hearty, and so no harm will come to him, even if it is a little heavy; and I'll make a hole in the bottom to feed my lord through."

"Do what you will, only take me there!"

An hour after, a wagon loaded with bricks and drawn by two horses left Uman. On one of them sat the tall Yankel, as long as a roadside sign, his long, curly locks waving from beneath his skull-cap as he bounced up and down on the horse.

CHAPTER ELEVEN

AT THE time when these events took place, there were as yet no custom-house officials or patrols on the frontiers—the terror of enterprising people—so that anyone could carry across anything he fancied. If anyone happened to make a search or inspection, it was but chiefly for his own pleasure, particularly if the wagon contained anything that excited the eye, and if his own hand possessed a certain weight and power. But the bricks tempted no one and were driven unhindered through the main gates of the city. From his narrow cage Bulba could only hear the noise of the streets and the shouts of the drivers. Bouncing up and down on his short, dusty steed, Yankel turned, after taking care to foul his trail, into a dark alley, which was called Dirty Street. This street was remarkably like a back yard turned wrong side out. The sun never seemed to shine over it. The time-blackened wooden houses and numerous poles projecting from the windows added to the darkness. Here and there a red brick wall stood out between the houses, but it, too, had already turned black in many places. Rarely did a bit of stuccoed wall gleam with a dazzling whiteness high up in the sunshine. Everything here offended the eye: chimneys, rags, rubbish, discarded pots and pans. Everyone flung into the street whatever was useless to him, abusing with every kind of refuse all the five senses of the passer-by. A man on horseback could almost reach with his hand the poles thrown across the street from one house to another, upon which dangled stockings, short pantaloons, or a smoked goose. At times, the small face of a rather pretty girl, adorned with discolored beads, peeped out of an ancient window. A crowd of brats, grimy, tattered, and curly-headed, shrieked and rolled in the mud. A red-haired man, with a face freckled as a sparrow's egg, looked out of a window and at once began to talk with Yankel in his gibberish; and Yankel drove into a yard. Another man, passing along the street, stopped and joined in their talk, and when Bulba finally crawled from under the bricks, he saw all three of them talking with great animation.

Yankel turned to him and said that all would be done, that his Ostap was in the city gaol, and thought it would be difficult to persuade the guards, yet he hoped to arrange a meeting for him.

Bulba went into a room together with the three men.

The men again began to talk among themselves in their unintelligible language. Taras looked at each of them. Something seemed to have excited him deeply: a powerful flame of hope flashed over his rough and stolid face—of hope such as sometimes visits a man reduced to the highest degree of despair; his old heart beat high, like that of a young man.

"Listen, men!" said he, and there was a note of exultation in his voice. "You can do anything, even to digging up the sea-bottom; and it has long been a proverb that the Jew can steal his own self if he chooses. Set my Ostap free! Help him to escape the devil's hands. To this man I have promised twelve thousand ducats; I will add another twelve thousand. All my costly goblets and buried gold, my house, and my last garment will I give you, and make a compact with you for my whole life to give you half of all I win in war."

"Oh, it cannot be done, sweet sir! it cannot be done!" said Yankel with a sigh.

"No, it cannot be done!" said another.

All three looked at one another.

"And if we try?" said the third, glancing timorously at the other two. "God may help us."

All three began talking in German. No matter how hard Bulba strained his ears, he could make nothing of it; all he heard was the oft-repeated word *Mardohai*.

"Listen, my lord!" said Yankel. "We must consult a man whose like never yet was in the world! Ooh! Ooh! He is as wise as Solomon; and when he cannot do something, nobody on earth can. Sit here; here is the key; let no one in!"

They went out into the street.

Taras locked the door and looked out of the little window upon the dirty street. The three stopped in the middle of the street and began to talk quite excitedly; they were soon joined by a fourth, and finally by a fifth. He again heard them repeat, *Mardohai, Mardohai*. They kept looking towards one end of the street, until at last a foot in a shoe and the skirts of a coat appeared from behind a ramshackle house at the corner. "Ah, Mardohai! Mardohai!" they all shouted at once. A gaunt man somewhat shorter than Yankel, but much more wrinkled, and with a huge upper lip, came up to the impatient group; and all of them hastened, in eager rivalry, to tell him of their business, while Mardohai glanced several times at the little window, from which Taras gathered that they were speaking about him. Mardohai waved his hands, listened, interrupted their speech, spat frequently aside, and, raising the skirts of his coat, thrust his hand into his pocket, and drew out some trinkets, displaying his foul pantaloons. At length, all of them set up such a screaming that the man who was standing on guard had to signal to them to be quiet, and Taras began to fear for his safety.

A minute or two later they entered the room all together. Mardohai went up to Bulba, patted him on the shoulder, and said, "When we and God set our minds on doing something, we always have our way."

Taras looked at this Solomon, whose like never yet was in the world, and was filled with new hope. Indeed, the appearance of the man inspired a certain amount of confidence: his upper lip was a monster, its thickness being doubtlessly increased by circumstances beyond his control. This Solomon's beard numbered only a dozen odd hairs, and those on the left side only. Solomon's face bore so many traces of blows, occasioned by his doughty deeds, that, in all probability, he had long lost count of them and took them as birthmarks.

Mardohai departed with his companions, who marvelled at his wisdom. Bulba was left alone. He was in a strange, unprecedented situation, and was filled with an anxiety he had never known before. His heart was in a fever. He was no longer the Bulba he had been—unbending, unshakable, strong as an oak; he was faint-hearted; he had grown weak. He started at every sound, at the glimpse of every figure that appeared at the end of the street. In this state he passed the whole day; he neither ate nor drank, and his eyes never left the little window. At last, at the close of the evening, Mardohai and Yankel appeared. Bulba's heart stopped beating.

"What? Is all well?" demanded he of them, with the impatience of a wild horse.

But even before they could muster enough courage to answer, he noticed that Mardohai had no longer his last temple-lock, which, though ungracefully, had curled from under his skull-cap. It was to be seen that he wished to say something, but instead he burst into such gibberish that Taras could not understand a word. Yankel himself kept clasping his hand to his mouth as if suffering from a cold.

"Oh, sweet sir!" said Yankel. "It cannot be done now! By God, it cannot! They are such bad people that one ought to spit on their very heads! Mardohai will tell you the same. And Mardohai has done what no other man could ever do, but God did not will that we should have our way. Three thousand soldiers are quartered here, and tomorrow the prisoners are all to be put to death."

Taras looked into the men's eyes, but no longer with impatience or anger.

"And if my lord would see him, then it must be done early tomorrow, even before sunrise. The guards are willing, and one of the chief wardens has given his promise. Only, may they know no happiness in the next world! Oh, woe is me! What a greedy people they are! Greedier, even, than any of us; I give fifty ducats to each, and to the chief warden—"

"Good. Take me to him!" Taras broke in resolutely, his heart again as stout as ever.

He agreed to Yankel's suggestion that he should disguise himself as a foreign count, just arrived from Germany, for which purpose the far-sighted merchant had already procured a costume.

It was already night. The master of the house—the red-haired, freckled man—dragged out a thin mattress covered with a mat and spread it on a bench for Bulba. Yankel lay upon the floor on another mattress of the same kind. The red-

111

haired man drank a small cup of some infusion, took off his coat, and, looking in his shoes and stockings like a chicken, repaired with his wife into another room. Two little children lay on the floor in the room like two house puppies. But Taras did not sleep; he sat motionless and drummed on the table with his fingers; he kept his pipe in his mouth and puffed out smoke, which made Yankel sneeze in his sleep and pull his blanket over his nose. Scarcely was the sky touched with the first pale glimmer of dawn when he pushed Yankel with his foot.

"Get up, man, and give me your count's dress!"

He was dressed in a moment; he blackened his mustachios and eyebrows, put a small dark cap on his head—and not even the Cossacks who knew him best would have recognized him. He seemed to be not more than thirty-five years old. A healthy flush glowed on his cheeks, and his scars somehow lent him an imperious air. The dress, adorned with gold, became him perfectly.

The streets were still asleep. Not a single mercantile creature, basket in hand, had yet appeared in the city. Bulba and Yankel came to a building that looked like a sitting stork. It was low, wide, huge, blackened, and on one side of it, craning upwards like a stork's neck, was a long slender turret, on the top of which part of a roof was to be seen. This building served many various purposes: here were barracks, a prison, and even a criminal court. Our travellers entered the gate and found themselves in a roomy hall, or covered court-yard. About a thousand men were sleeping here. Straight before them was a low door, in front of which sat two sentries playing at a game which consisted in one beating the other's palm with two fingers. They paid scant attention to the newcomers, and turned their heads only when Yankel said, "It's us. D'you hear, sirs? It's us."

"Go in!" said one of them, opening the door with one hand and holding out the other for his comrade to rap.

They stepped into a narrow and dark passage, which led them to a hall like the first, with small windows overhead.

"Who goes there?" shouted several voices, and Taras beheld a large number of soldiers, heavily armed. "We have orders not to let anyone pass!"

"It's us," shouted Yankel. "By heavens, it's us, noble sirs!"

But no one would listen to him. Fortunately, a stout man came up at that moment, who seemed, by his appearance, to be the chief there, for he swore more lustily than all the others.

"My lord, it's us! You know us already; and his lordship, the count, will thank you once more."

"Let them pass, a hundred devils and Satan's mother! And admit no one else. And do not take off your swords and lie like dogs on the floor. . . ."

The conclusion of this eloquent order our travellers did not hear.

"It's us . . . it's me . . . it's friends!" Yankel kept saying to everyone they met.

"May we go in now?" he asked one of the guards, when they at last reached the end of the passage.

"Yes; but I don't know whether they'll let you pass into the prison itself. Jan is no longer there; another has taken his place."

"Oh, oh!" muttered Yankel softly. "This looks bad, sweet sir!"

"Go on!" said Taras stubbornly.

The man obeyed.

At the door of the dungeon, set in a lancet arch, stood a soldier with a three-storied moustache; the upper story went backwards, the second straight forward, and the third down-wards, which made him greatly resemble a tom-cat.

The merchant hunched his back as much as he could and sidled up to him.

"Your excellency! Most illustrious lord!"

"Do you speak to me, pig?"

"To you, most illustrious lord!"

"Hm, but I'm nothing but a common soldier!" said the guard, his eyes glittering with delight.

"By heavens—I thought it was the chief himself! Ah, how important he looks! Like a colonel, by heavens! A hairs-breadth more, and he would be a colonel! My lord ought to be placed on a horse as swift as a fly, and put in command of regiments!"

The soldier stroked the lower story of his mustaches, his eyes glittering brighter than ever with delight.

"What fine people the military are!" continued Yankel. "Oh, dear me! what good people! The braid and the trappings—they shine like the sun. And the maidens, whenever they see military men—oh, oh!"

The soldier twirled his upper mustachios and uttered a

sound through his teeth much like the neighing of a horse.

"I beg my lord to do us a service," said Yankel. "Here is a prince, come from a foreign land, who wishes to look at the Cossacks. He has never in all his life seen what manner of men are the Cossacks."

Foreign counts and barons were no uncommon thing in Poland; they were often drawn there by mere curiosity to see this half-Asiatic corner of Europe—they regarded Muscovy and the Ukraine as part of Asia. So the soldier bowed low, and thought fit to say a few words of his own accord.

"I do not know, your excellency," said he, "why you should want to look at them. They are dogs, not men. And their faith is such as no one respects."

"You lie, you devil's son!" said Bulba. "You are a dog yourself. How dare you say that our faith is not respected? It is your heretical faith that is not respected!"

"Aha!" said the soldier. "I know who you are, my friend: you yourself are one of those I am guarding here. Wait till I call our men here!"

Taras saw his blunder now; but obstinacy and vexation prevented him from finding a means of repairing it. Fortunately, Yankel came to his rescue at once.

"Most illustrious lord! How is it possible that a count can be a Cossack? And were he a Cossack, where could he have got such a costume and a count's mien?"

"None of your lies now!" And the soldier opened his wide mouth to shout.

"Your royal majesty! Be quiet! be quiet! For heaven's sake!" shouted Yankel. "We'll reward you for it as no one has ever been rewarded: we will give you two gold ducats!"

"Ha! Two ducats! Two ducats are nothing to me: I give my barber two ducats for shaving only half my beard. Give me a hundred ducats, pit!" Here the soldier twirled his upper mustachios. "If you don't give me a hundred ducats at once, I'll shout out!"

"Why must he have so much!" sorrowfully said Yankel, turning pale; he untied his leather purse, and rejoiced that he had no more there, and that the soldier was unable to count over a hundred.

"My lord, let us go at once! You see what bad people they are here!" said Yankel, noting that the soldier was turning the money over in his hand with an air of regret at not having demanded more.

"How so? You devil!" said Bulba. "You've taken the money, and will not show me the Cossacks? No, you must show them. You cannot refuse now that you've taken the money."

"Go, go to the devil! If you don't, I'll call out this minute, and you'll— Begone, I tell you!"

"My lord! My lord! In heaven's name, let us go! A plague upon them! May they dream of things that shall make them spit!" shouted poor Yankel.

Bulba turned round slowly, with bent head, and went back, Yankel following him and heaping reproaches upon him, for he was sorely put out by the loss of the wasted ducats.

"Oh, woe is me! What luck God sends to people! A hundred ducats merely for driving us away! And we—they tear off our hair and work on our faces till you cannot bear to look at them, and nobody gives us a hundred ducats! Oh, my God! My merciful God!"

But their failure made a much deeper impression on Bulba, as was shown by a devouring flame in his eyes.

"Let us go!" said he suddenly, as though arousing himself. "Let us go to the square. I want to see how they will torture him."

"Oh, my lord! Why do you wish to go? We cannot help him now."

"We will go!" said Bulba stubbornly.

And, like a nurse, Yankel sighed and dragged himself after him.

The square on which the execution was to take place was not hard to find: crowds of people were thronging there from all quarters. In that rough age such a sight was an attractive spectacle not only for the rabble, but also for the upper classes. A host of the most pious old women, a number of the most cowardly young maidens and ladies, who would afterwards dream of nothing but bloody corpses all night long and shriek in their sleep as loudly as any drunken hussar, would never miss an opportunity of indulging their curiosity. "Ah, what tortures!" many of them would cry in a hysterical fever, shutting their eyes and turning away, but, nevertheless, they would stand out the show to the end. Some, with gaping mouths and outstretched hands, would have liked to jump upon the heads of those in front of them to get a better view. Among the crowd of narrow, small, and ordinary heads, the fat face of a butcher might be seen, who watched the whole process with the air of a connoisseur and conversed in monosyllables with an armorer, whom he called his foster brother because he used to get drunk with him in the same pot-house on holidays. Some vehemently commented on all they saw, others even laid wagers, but most of the crowd were such as watch the world, and all that happens on earth, stolidly picking their noses.

In the foreground, close to the heavily mustached soldiers of the city guard, stood a young gentleman, or one who tried to pass for a gentleman, in a military dress, who had evidently put on the entire contents of his wardrobe, leaving only a torn shirt and a pair of old boots at his quarters. Two chains, one above the other, hung around his neck, supporting something that looked like a ducat. He stood beside his sweetheart, Izefa, and kept glancing about every moment to see that no one soiled her silk dress. He explained everything to her in such minute detail that there was decidedly nothing anyone might have added.

"All these people whom you see here, my darling Izefa," said he, "have come to see the criminals executed. And that man, darling, whom you see there holding an axe and other instruments in his hands, is the executioner, and he is going to torture them, and put them to death. When he breaks any one of them on the wheel and tortures him in other ways, the criminal will still be alive; but when he cuts off his head, darling, he will die at once. Before that, he will yell and kick; but as soon as his head is chopped off, he will neither yell, nor eat, nor drink, because, darling, he will no longer have any head."

Izefa listened to all this with awe and curiosity.

The house-tops were crowded with people. From the dormer-windows peered strange mustachioed faces, with bonnet-like caps on their heads. On the canopied balconies sat the aristocracy. The lovely hand of a laughing lady, brilliant as white sugar, rested on a railing. Illustrious nobles—stout gentlemen they were—looked on with an air of dignity. A lackey in rich garb, with hanging sleeves, carried round various refreshments. Often, a black-eyed roguish damsel would pick up cake or fruit with her lily hand, and fling it into the throng beneath. The crowd of hungry cavaliers held up their caps to catch it, and some tall squire, whose head towered above the others, in a faded red coat with tarnished gold braid, would be the first to seize it with his long arms, kiss

116

his prize, hold it to his heart, and then dispatch it into his mouth. A falcon in a golden cage, hanging under a balcony, was also a spectator; with head bent to one side, and with one foot raised, he, too, looked attentively down at the crowd. Suddenly the crowd became noisier, and voices were heard on all sides. "They are bringing them! They are bringing the Cossacks!"

They came with their long scalp-locks uncovered, their beards unshaven. They came neither timidly nor gloomily, but with a quiet pride; their garments of costly cloth were worn out and hung in tatters; they did not look at nor bow to the crowd. In front of all came Ostap.

What were old Bulba's feelings when he saw his Ostap? What was in his heart? He gazed at him from amidst the crowd, and lost not a single movement of his. Ostap halted. He was to drink the bitter cup before any of them. He looked at his comrades, raised his hand, and said loudly, "God grant that the impious heretics, as many as stand here, may not hear a Christian suffer! that none of us may utter a single word!"

After that he stepped up to the scaffold.

"Well said, son! Well said!" said Bulba softly and cast down his grey head.

The executioner tore off Ostap's tatters; his hands and feet were lashed to specially made stocks, and—. But we will not distress the Reader by a picture of the hellish tortures, which would make his hackles rise. They were the outcome of those coarse, savage times, when man still lived a life of bloody military exploits that hardened his soul, which was almost a complete stranger to human feeling. In vain did a few men, who were exceptions in that epoch, oppose these terrible measures. In vain did the king and many knights, enlightened in mind and soul, point out that such cruelty of punishment could but inflame the revengefulness of the Cossack nation. But the power of royalty and of wise counsel was as nothing before the lawlessness and arrogant will of the country's magnates, who turned the Parliament into a mere satire on government by reason of their thoughtlessness, inconceivable and utter lack of foresight, childish conceit, and petty hauteur.

Ostap bore the torments and tortures like a giant. Not a cry, not a groan was heard even when they began to break the bones in his arms and legs; when the remotest spectators

117

heard their horrible cracking amidst the deathlike hush that gripped the crowd; when the ladies turned their eyes away. Not a single groan escaped his lips, not a single muscle twitched in his face. Taras stood in the crowd with bowed head, but his eyes were raised proudly, and he repeated approvingly, "Well done, son! Well done!"

But when they dragged him to the last tortures of death, it seemed as though his strength was giving way. He cast his eyes around. God! Only strange, unknown faces! If only but one dear soul had been here to witness his death! He would not have wished to hear the sobs and sorrow of his weak mother, nor the wild shrieks of a wife, tearing her hair and beating her white breasts; he would have wished now to see a firm man, whose wise word might bring him fresh strength and solace in death's hour. And his strength failed him, and he cried in the agony of his soul, "Batko! Where are you? Do you hear me?"

"I hear you!" rang through the universal silence, and the million people there shuddered as one man.

A party of mounted guards rushed to comb the throng. Yankel turned pale as death, and as soon as the horsemen had ridden past him, he looked round in terror for Taras; but Taras was no longer behind him; not a trace of him was left.

CHAPTER TWELVE

BUT TRACES of Taras were not lost. A Cossack army of a hundred and twenty thousand men appeared on the borders of the Ukraine. This was no longer a small party or detachment sallying forth for plunder or in pursuit of the Tatars. No: the whole nation had arisen, for the people's patience was at an end. It had arisen to avenge the violation of its rights; the shameful humiliation of its customs; the profanation of the faith of its fathers and its holy rites; the desecration of its churches; the outrages of the foreign lords; its oppression; the Papal Union; all that had so long nourished and embittered the stern hatred of the Cossacks.

Hetman Ostranitsa, young but strong of heart, was the leader of the numberless Cossack host. Beside him was Gunya, his old and experienced comrade-in-arms, and counsellor. Eight colonels led the regiments, each twelve thousand strong. Two general esauls and a general standard-bearer rode behind the hetman. The general standard-bearer carried the chief standard; many other standards and banners floated in the distance behind, as well as horse-tails nailed to poles. There were many other officers in the foot and horse regiments: baggage-masters, lieutenants, regimental scriveners; besides the registered Cossacks, there was almost an equal number of volunteers, on foot and on horse-back. The Cossacks had risen everywhere; they came from Chigirin and Pereyaslav, from Baturin and Glukhov, and from the lower and upper reaches of the Dnieper, and from all its islands. Countless horses and wagons stretched across the fields. And among all these Cossacks, among all the eight regiments, one was the choicest; and that was the regiment led by Taras Bulba. Everything marked him above the others; his ripe years, his experience, his skill in commanding his troops, and his surpassing hatred of the foe. Even the Cossacks thought his ruthless fierceness and cruelty excessive. His grey head adjudged nothing but the stake and gallows, and his counsel at the councils of war breathed nought save extermination.

It would be out of place to describe here all the battles in which the Cossacks showed their prowess, or the progress of the campaign: all this is inscribed on the pages of chronicles. It is well known what a war waged for the faith is like in Russia; there is no power stronger than faith. It is unconquerable and formidable like a rock, not made by human hands, in the midst of a stormy, ever-changing sea. From the deep bed of the sea it rears its unbreakable monolithic walls. It is seen from every point, and looks the passing waves straight in the face. And woe to the ship that dashes against it! Her fragile riggings fly in splinters, everything in her is crushed and drowned, and the startled air is rent by the piteous shrieks of her perishing crew.

The pages of the chronicles record in detail how the Polish garrisons fled from the towns freed by the Cossacks; how all the rapacious usurers were hanged; how powerless was the Royal Hetman Mikolaj Potocki with his great army against this invincible force; how, routed and pursued, he lost the best part of his army in a wretchedly small stream; how the dreaded Cossack regiments besieged him in the little town of Polonnoye; and how, reduced to the last extremity, the Polish hetman promised, under oath, in the name of the king and his ministers, to satisfy all their demands and to restore all their former rights and privileges. But the Cossacks were not to be taken in by this: they knew the worth of a Polish oath. And Potocki would never more have pranced on his six-thousand-ducat steed, attracting the glances of high-born ladies and the envy of the cavaliers; never more would he have graced the Parliament and given sumptuous feasts to the senators—had not the Russian priests of the town saved his life. When all the priests, in their brilliant gold mantles, went out to meet them, bearing the icons and crosses, led by the bishop himself, crosier in hand and a pastoral mitre on his head, all the Cossacks bowed their heads and took off their caps. To no one, not even the king, would they have shown respect at that hour, but they dared not rebel against their own Christian Church, and obeyed their priests. The hetman and his colonels agreed to set Potocki free, having made him solemnly vow to leave all the Christian churches unmolested, to let bygones be bygones, and do no harm to Cossack chivalry. One colonel alone would not consent to such a peace. It was Taras. He tore a tuft of hair from his head and cried, "Hey, generals and colonels! Do no such woman's deed! Trust not the Poles; they will betray us, the dogs!"

And when a regimental scrivener presented the terms, and the general signed them with his own hand, Taras took off his rich Turkish sabre with a blade of damask steel, broke it in twain like a reed, and flung each half in opposite directions, saying:

"Farewell! As those halves will never meet and make one blade, so we, comrades, shall never again see each other in this world. Remember my parting words!" Here his voice swelled and rose higher, ringing with a hitherto unknown power; and all shuddered to hear the prophetic words: "At the hour of your death will you remember me! You think you have bought peace and quiet? You think you will now have it? Not so: others will lord over you. You, general, shall have your head skinned, stuffed with buckwheat bran, and long will it be made a show at every fair. Neither will you, gentlemen, save your heads! You will languish in damp dungeons, behind stone walls, if you are not boiled in cauldrons like sheep! And you, my lads," he went on, turning to his own men, "which of you wants to die a natural death—not wallowing on your couches or on women's beds, not drunk under a hedge near a pot-house, like carrion, but a true Cossack death—all in one bed, like bride and groom? Or, perhaps, you would like to return home, and turn infidels, and carry Polish priests on your backs?"

"We follow you, Colonel! We follow you!" cried all who were in Bulba's regiment, and many others went over to them.

"If so, then follow me!" said Taras, ramming his cap unto

his brows and glaring at those who stayed behind. He settled himself in his saddle and shouted to his men, "May we be remembered by no unkind word! Come on, lads! We'll pay the Catholics a visit!"

With this he whipped his horse, and there followed him a long train of a hundred wagons, and many Cossacks, horse and foot; and turning, he glared at those who stayed behind, and his eyes were full of wrath. None dared to stop him. The regiment left in sight of the whole army, and long did Taras turn round and glare.

The general and the colonels stood downcast; all became thoughtful and were silent for a long time, as though oppressed by gloomy forebodings. Taras had not prophesied in vain: all came to pass as he had prophesied. Very soon, after the betrayal at Kanev, the general's head, together with those of many of his chief officers, was stuck up on a pole.

And what of Taras? Taras rode deep into Poland with his regiment, burned eighteen towns and forty Papist churches, and reached Cracow itself. Many nobles did he kill, many of the best and richest castles did he plunder; his Cossacks unsealed and poured out on the ground the century-old wine and mead, carefully stored in lordly cellars; they hacked and burned the costly articles, garments, and everything they found in the storerooms. "Spare nothing!" was all Taras said. No mercy did the Cossacks show to the black-browed ladies, to the white-bosomed, pearly-faced maidens; not even at the altar could they save themselves: Taras burned them, altars and all. More than one pair of snow-white hands were raised to heaven from amidst the fiery flames, with piteous shrieks, which would have moved the cold earth itself and caused the steppe-grass to bend in pity. But the cruel Cossacks paid heed to nothing, and, lifting the children in the streets on the points of their spears, they threw them also into the flames.

"This is Ostap's funeral feast, you infernal Poles!" was all Taras said. And such funeral feasts in Ostap's memory he held in every town and village, until the Polish government saw that his acts were more than ordinary robber raids, and the same Potocki, with five regiments, was ordered to capture him without fail.

Six days did the Cossacks successfully evade their pursuers, fleeing along country tracks; though their horses could hardly bear up under the strain of this unusual flight, they almost succeeded in saving them. But this time Potocki was equal to the task entrusted him; unceasingly he pursued them and overtook them on the bank of the Dniester, where Taras had camped for rest in an abandoned and ruined fortress.

On the very brink of a steep cliff above the Dniester loomed its shattered ramparts and crumbling walls. Rubble and broken bricks covered the top of the cliff, which seemed to be ready at any moment to break and hurtle down. Here it was, on its two sides facing the plain, that the Royal Hetman Potocki surrounded Bulba. Four days did the Cossacks fight, repulsing the Poles with bricks and stones. But at last their strength and provisions gave out, and Taras resolved to fight his way through the enemy ranks. And the Cossacks would have fought their way through, and their swift horses might again have served them faithfully, had not Taras halted suddenly, in the very heat of their fight, and shouted, "Wait! I've dropped my pipe. Not even my pipe and tobacco will the infernal Poles have!" And the old ataman stooped down and began to search in the grass for his pipe, his constant companion over land and sea, in his campaigns and at home. Just then a hand of soldiers rushed up and seized him by his mighty shoulders. He tried to shake himself free, but no longer as of old did the soldiers fall down around him. "Ah, old age, old age!" he said, and the stout old Cossack wept. But it was not old age at all; simply, the strength of one man had yielded to the strength of many. Well nigh thirty men clung to his arms and legs. "We've caught our bird!" shrieked the Poles. "Now we must think how to give the dog his due!" With their general's leave, they resolved to burn him alive in the sight of all. Near at hand stood the bare trunk of a tree, whose top had been struck off by lightning. They fastened him with iron chains to the trunk and drove nails into his hands; the Cossack was raised on high, so that he might be seen from afar; beneath, they piled faggots. But Taras did not look down on them, nor did he think about the fire with which they were about to burn him; he gazed, poor fellow, in the direction where his Cossacks were firing back at their pursuers; from the height to which he had been lifted, he could see them as clearly as if they were in the palm of his hand.

"Quick, lads, reach that hill!" cried he. "That hill beyond the wood: they will not take you there!"

But the wind did not carry his words to them.

"They're lost! Lost! And all for a trifle!" he said in despair and looked down at the sparkling Dniester.

Joy flashed in his eyes; he saw the prows of four boats projecting out of a clump of bushes. Gathering all the power of his lungs, he shouted at the top of his voice:

"To the bank, lads! To the bank! Take the downhill path on the left! There are boats near the bank—take them all, or they'll chase you!"

This time the wind blew from the other side, and all his words were caught by the Cossacks. But this advice cost him a blow on the head with the back of an axe, which made everything turn over in his eyes.

The Cossacks galloped down the cliff path at full speed, but their pursuers were already treading upon their heels, and they saw that the path twisted and zig-zagged, checking their flight. "Here goes, comrades!" said they; all pulled up for a moment, raised their whips, whistled, and their Tatar horses, springing from the ground, stretched themselves snakelike in the air, flew over the precipice, and plunged into the Dniester. Only two riders failed to reach the river, but crashed down from the height upon the rocks, and perished there with their horses without uttering a cry. But the Cossacks were already swimming with the horses and unfastening the boats. The Poles stopped on the brink of the precipice, marvelling at the unheard-of Cossack feat, and uncertain whether to jump down or not. One hot-blooded young colonel, the brother of the beautiful Pole who had bewitched poor Andrei, did not stop to think long, but with might and main leaped with his horse after the Cossacks—only to crash down on the rocks. Torn to pieces by the sharp stones, he perished in the abyss, and his brains, mingled with blood, splashed the bushes that grew on the rough wall of the chasm.

When Taras Bulba recovered from the blow and glanced at the Dniester, the Cossacks were already rowing away in the boats, balls were showered from above, but fell short of them. And the old ataman's eyes sparkled with joy.

"Farewell, comrades!" he called to them from above. "Remember me, and come hither again next spring for another glorious raid! How now, you infernal Poles? Think ye there is aught in the world that can daunt a Cossack? Wait! The day will come when you shall learn what the Orthodox Russian is! Already do peoples far and near forbode it: there shall arise a ruler from Russian soil, and there shall be no power on earth that shall not yield to him!"

The flames rose from the wood, gripping his feet and running up the tree. . . . But what fire, what torture, what power can be found on earth that can overpower Russian power!

The Dniester is no small river, and many are its backwaters, dense rushes, shallows, and deep holes. Its mirror-like surface glitters, and over it ring the cries of the swan, and the proud river-duck glides swiftly over it, and many are the snipe and red-throated ruffs and other birds that hide in its reeds and along its banks. The Cossacks rowed on, swiftly and steadily, in their narrow double-ruddered boats, steering clear of the shoals, startling the birds. They rowed on and talked of their *ataman.*

If your dealer does not have any of the MAGNUM EASY EYE CLASSICS, send price of book plus 10 cents to cover postage to MAGNUM CLASSICS, 18 East 41st Street, Room 1501, New York, N.Y. 10017.